By Adrienne Nash

'Trudi'
'Trudi in Paris'
'Trudi and Simon'
'Trudi without Simon'

'Wide Skies' a history of the Norfolk and Norwich Art Circle, with statistics by Brian Watts.

'A Strange Life' an autobiography

Crime novels
'The Cellar'
'A Time to be Brave'

Trudi in Paris

By

Adrienne Nash

Chapter 1.

Hi, my name is Trudi My name was given to me when I was eight by Heather, a neighbour's daughter. That really is another story.

I am just eighteen, and I am now complete as a woman at last, except that I have never had sex with a man, well, not in the traditional baby making way. That is something I look forward to in the future. I am, some say, beautiful but I always think there is a degree of flattery there. I look in the mirror and see someone that apparently no one else does. Nevertheless, on a good day when I have completed my makeup, my reflection is affable and smiles back at me.

I certainly do have brains, my final school exams attest to that. I had a place at Cambridge University and I am off to university, not Cambridge as I had planned, but the Sorbonne in Paris to study medicine. Yes, that is a very strange decision, but there is a good reason.

Sam, my dearest girl friend from school days is to stay in Paris with me for the first month or so while I settle in. At one time her brother and I were very attracted to each other. That romance came to nothing, much to Sam's disappointment. There are of course good reasons. I was sixteen, he was twenty-one. I looked like an attractive schoolgirl, white blouse, purple blazer, grey pleated skirt three inches above my knee. However we both knew that I was not ready. Nor would I ever be able to give him babies. So you see, however much my appearance and my vivacious nature dazzled him, I was essentially an illusion.

Michael is now engaged to a lovely Italian girl he met in Venice while staying in the family villa in Punta Sabbioni across the lagoon from Venice.

Now I am at last whole, thank god. I feel as though I have been delivered from imminent death. The relief at being the new me, equates to that felt by a rock climber who sees the rope he is suspended from, starting to fray, and just in time, manages to land on solid rock and haul himself to safety.

Sam is now unattached like me, so we look forward to an exciting life in Paris before my course at the Pierre and Marie Curie Faculty begins.

Sam arrived at my parents' house the last week in August. In her gap year she is sort of trying out Paris, then going to New York as an intern and I think going to teach in

Malawi before University in a year's time. Sam proved a faithful companion at school where as you might expect, I was subject of considerable interest and bullying.

We had two days at my home before we packed my little Mini Cooper, the real one not that BMW travesty so beloved of young women. It was Father mostly did the packing of my essential possessions. He is good at that sort of thing, making order out of chaos. I think I have inherited that trait too. Mother is putting on a brave face, but tears are near the surface. Even father has expressed concern, but they have both met Simon who they consider will be in loco parentis. Simon had phoned to say that my apartment in his Paris mansion is ready, so we can set off and settle in. After being accepted by the Sorbonne to study medicine, I decided to take Simon's offer of a free flat, a small allowance and some intermittent modelling, so the burden of a medical education will not fall on my parents.

Oh, I forgot in my excitement. You don't know Simon. Well we have quite a history. I first met him three years ago in Normandy where he has a gorgeous Château. He is rich and he is sixteen years older than me.

OK, I had better tell you all about Simon. Just as Vanessa in the last instalment of my life, was fairy godmother, Simon is my fairy godfather, easing all my difficulties. Simon de Beauvonne is cultured, a man of the World, who knows about fashion, music, art, theatre and food. He saw potential in me and even paid for this poor androgynous hermaphrodite to make the change, partly because his younger brother had been like me, but after being rejected by the family, had fallen into vice and committed suicide.

Simon's money and contacts cracked open the chrysalis and allowed the butterfly to unfold her wings. I love him and I believe he loves me. I hope he does. Property of Comte de Beauvonne, I would have it tattooed across my wrist if he asked me to do so, even though I hate tattoos. Nothing to me is as beautiful as human skin. It has been he who has set up my entrance to the Sorbonne and he who financed my surgery in San Francisco, so I owe him a great debt of gratitude, not that he seeks any reward.

Of course it was not just a consideration of the expense of University, but my love of Paris and the exotic fashion trade that convinced me to reject Cambridge in favour of the Sorbonne. What a hard choice to make. No, that is not the full truth either. Above all it was my deep love for Simon, owner amongst other things of the haute couture House of Beauvonne and a château in Normandy. I was introduced to him by Ellie, the daughter of my 'fairy godmother,' Vanessa. The latter knew the fashion world intimately having been a top model in the eighties. I have walked the catwalk as a model for Simon twice, but the press sensationalised our association, inferring that he was having an affair with a transvestite. If my birth and the press are not enough difficulties for us, he also needs heirs, and for that he needs a wife to bear children.

For these reasons, he is living with his PR guru, Catherine Schûster, and I hear that they will marry. OK, so it has all been a dream of ours that we would be together, or maybe just my dream. The practical difficulties for someone in his position are almost insurmountable. But for me, I will never live down the fact that I was born with the wrong body. It makes little difference to my day-to-day life, but for a man in the centre of the public eye and one who needs a partner to give him heirs, it is another matter.

You can tell already that he is my idol, my obsession. Yes he is much older than me and while he wants babies to inherit his empire he wants me to find myself too. He has not asked me to wait for him, nor placed any restrictions on me. Indeed, he has said that I should enjoy student life to the full, with all that involves, but I do find it difficult thinking of him with Catherine. On the other hand, as a transsexual woman,

I will never be able to bear children for him and what he needs above all is an heir to his estates and fortune. He is the dearest man. So there are no strings in our association.

It was a fine early September day when Sam and I said goodbye to my tearful parents and set off for Dieppe in my Mini.

The journey to Paris was my first long drive since passing my test and I was glad to have Sam as a companion. We had decided to take the Newhaven to Dieppe ferry because of a cheap offer and because the drive from Dieppe to Paris was shorter, as was the distance from my home in south Surrey to Newhaven. We were soon on the A22, bowling through Sussex. Father told mother that I am a good driver, but actually I don't agree. I have had several near misses that I don't talk about, and I have only been driving for four months, so having Sam to restrain me and to navigate is a real boon. Even so, we missed the dock gate and amid giggles had to reverse, narrowly missing an invisible to me, bus, so you see!

We arrived at Newhaven with forty-five minutes before the sailing at 11.00 am and more or less drove straight on board. We decided to have lunch on the ship as we had a four-hour voyage. We shared a half bottle of champagne to celebrate our exam results and our holiday together. It was all very exciting, even though I had lived rather a high life in the last two years.

The sea was smooth, the meal, a salad buffet, scrumptious and we were relaxed. The crossing was completely uneventful and we were soon trundling on to the French dock and out of Dieppe. I managed to remember to drive on the right, and it was surprisingly easy to adapt. By 18.30 we arrived at the villa off Boulevard Haussmann. All the dire warnings about the standard of French driving proved false. Paris was no worse than South London. The sat nav given as a parting present by my parents proved invaluable.

Sam pressed the electronic key Simon had given me and the huge iron gate rolled back and we drove through to the underground garage and the space left for me.

We were unloading the car as the lift door opened and Madame Gameau the housekeeper and Simon's chauffeur Jerome, Madame's husband, emerged to welcome us and help with our baggage.

'Bonsoir Mlle Trudi.' She kissed me on both cheeks, then turned to Sam. I introduced Sam and we both shook hands with Jerome her husband and sometime chauffeur.

Madame Gameau took us up to the apartment, leaving us to explore. To my surprise, I had two bedrooms, as well as a large lounge/dining room. The seating end of the room looked out onto the courtyard garden at the rear, and faced southwest. The evening sun streamed through the window on to the classic modern furniture, creamy white suite and walls.

The room featured, as the estate agents say, a large statement abstract painting on the long wall in blue and red. A huge mirror above the white and pink marble fireplace completed the decor. Even the carpet was white, so I would have to be careful. On a sideboard there were two Royal Copenhagen figurines and a large fruit bowl also in the pale blue and white Copenhagen. I examined the figurines and found that the female was Virgo, for my birthday and the male Pisces for Simon. That gave me hope that he really did love me.

A huge bowl of lilies stood on a pedestal in the corner to the left of the large window and a bookshelf stood in the opposite corner. It contained a Larousse Illustré, French dictionary. An English medical dictionary and a French one, and also a Grey's Anatomy of the Human Body and several other medical books.

There were also several novels, English and French and a leather bound Dickens collection and another of Jane Austen. Simon had obviously put a lot of thought into the furnishing.

My bedroom contained a king size four-poster, but the curtains were light flowered printed silk rather than heavy drapes. The en suite was modern, marble tiled, floor and walls with a large mirror. I looked for wardrobes but found none then opened what appeared to be a cupboard. It proved to be a large walk in wardrobe, and was already filled with clothes, dresses, trousers and tops, underwear and shoes, bags and scarves, everything a society girl could want, even a whole rack of cosmetics in a range of colours. I cried. Sam stood open mouthed.

'Wow! I think someone really loves you.'

Sam's room was also nicely furnished with a queen size bed and another en suite.

The kitchen was small, a galley, but in white and black marble and fully equipped with machines. I was quite overwhelmed and Sam threw her arms around me.

'You deserve it,' she said, 'after all you have been through. I wish I were now starting university here.'

'That must be why he has given me two bedrooms, in case you come here.' I replied.

We unpacked and showered. As I emerged in a towel, the phone rang. It was Simon.

'Dearest Simon. I cannot believe you have done all this for me. It is just wonderful. How can I ever thank you?'

'Il n'y a rien,' he said. 'Francais maintenant. (French now).'

He was in Paris and was waiting to take us to dinner. Tomorrow he was flying to Tokyo, so this was my only chance to see him.

I yelled Sam and told her the plan for the evening. We had half an hour to get ready. I chose a light blue cocktail dress and stiletto sling backs to match and a sequinned evening bag. I allowed Sam the run of my wardrobe and she chose an emerald dress that set off her dark curls.

We met Simon in the lift. He hugged me so tightly I thought he would snap my spine. He kissed me on both cheeks and then on my lips. I felt quite faint. He released me too soon, so that he could speak to Sam. We stepped out into the street to a waiting taxi. We arrived at Chez Françoise in the Place de l'Alma and were ushered to a table behind a glass screen. Le Tour Eiffel its illuminations twinkling, was silhouetted against the dying embers of the setting sun.

Simon sat beside me with Sam opposite. Sam said that she was Jewish, so could not eat certain foods, although she rarely went to synagogue. Simon nodded and translated items on the menu for her to choose. He said that his family also had Jewish blood. I allowed Simon to choose for me.

We started with a bottle of champagne, Pol Roger, not Winston Churchill, but an excellent wine Simon assured us, and ate les amuse-bouches, ballotins and tapenades. Simon asked Sam what she was going to do in her gap year?

'I'm spending two months in Malawi, teaching, then because I want to be in finance, I am going to New York as an intern for another two.'

'Then you should return here to look after my Trudi.'

'I will be a frequent visitor if she will have me. But she will be wrestling with learning medicine in a foreign language. It will not be easy.'

'I will manage. You know you are always welcome here Sam. What could I wish for more, than to live in this great city, with the two people dearest to me.'

We settled to eating. I had lobster salad followed by tournados Rossini. I have no idea what they ate, my thoughts were in a whirl. I was surprised and gratified that Simon wanted Sam to keep an eye on me. He really did care as Vanessa had said, but was it as a lover or as a brother?

By eleven we were home. Simon gave me the key that unlocked the door between my apartment and his.

'I go to Tokyo tomorrow with Catherine,' he said, and I shuddered inwardly. 'I need to speak to you in private if Sam will excuse us. Come to my salon presently.'

I said my goodnight to Sam, and made my way through the locked door. I found Simon sitting his hands clenched before him, his face pained. I had thought at dinner that he was restrained and preoccupied, and I could see that I had been right.

'Come, sit by me,' he said.

I sat, knees folded under me, next to him on the soft old leather sofa. He took my hand and held it tight.

'You have to know that I love you, above anything or anyone.'

'But do you love me as a woman or the brother you lost?'

'Do you need to ask that? You are all woman to me. You always have been since our first meeting at that fancy dress party. This is why I have to tell you things that will appear in the newspapers so that you know the truth. I would like if you will be silent, so I can organise my thoughts. It is very difficult.

'You will hear next week that Catherine Schûster and I are to marry. No do not cry, please, or I cannot explain all. Catherine has agreed to marry me and to bare my children. It is a business agreement and legal. She will remain married in name for eight years and then we will divorce. I hope by then that we will have three children. She is now pregnant, it was confirmed yesterday and it is a boy. All that is good. In the meantime, you are here, where I want you to be and you must live your life as you want, including experimenting with men and your friends. I do know that you had an affair with Eleanor, and if that is what you want too, OK. I cannot ask you to be faithful while I am in a marriage even if it is a sham. Catherine and I do love each other in a sort of way, but not in the way I love you.

'You and I once discussed having an heir. Well this solves that problem. I will see you when in Paris, but sometimes Catherine will be with me. En France, such arrangements are not uncommon. As far as the press are concerned, you are my protégé. Can you do this, this pretence?'

'You know Simon that I do love you. It will hurt to see you with Catherine, but I am so lucky in my position to have you at all. I will do my best to live in a way that does not hurt or embarrass you. You know that. So this is a sort of goodbye?'

'A long au revoir as far as being a lover is concerned.'

'Then as a parting lover, I have a request, and you cannot refuse me.'

'Of course, anything dearest Trudi. Comment?'

'I want to sleep with you tonight. I want you to be my first lover as well as eventually, my last.'

'Are you sure you are ready? I do not want to hurt you.'

I rose from the sofa and held out my hand to him. 'Come, we will see. But I do not want to wait years and then you are disappointed in what you find. I just need to get some things first.'

I went to my apartment to find Sam sat reading in the lounge. 'Well?' she asked.

'All is well. I will tell you tomorrow.' Suddenly I felt embarrassed that Sam would know exactly what I was doing. Then logic took hold and I decided to be straightforward with her. 'I am going to stay with Simon tonight.'

I changed into my best nightdress and negligee, used some KY and was ready to see what would happen with my new anatomy. My heart was thumping in my chest and a small voice inside was whining, 'please don't let him be disappointed'.

Simon was already in his bedroom but still dressed.

'Are you sure dearest Trudi?'

'Oh yes. Of course, but do not expect to sleep much.'

He dimmed the lights and let the curtains fall around his four poster, and began to undress. There is nothing so funny to me as a man standing in shirt, under pants and socks. I smiled and giggled and he looked up in alarm.

'Are my legs so funny?' he asked.

I shook my head as I went towards him. I let the negligee fall as I walked, and wriggled out of the nightie, revealing my full body to him for the first time. I unbuttoned his shirt, wrenching the last button so that it pinged across the room. I slipped my fingers inside his underwear and lowered them, pulling them off his feet with his socks, while he hopped from one leg to the other. I stayed on my knees, looking up at his body. To my surprise, I saw a man much more muscular than I had thought, his skin tanned. He was not so hairy, just enough to look masculine.

His penis was at face level to me and stood fully erect, purple headed and throbbed with each beat of his heart. My brother's words to me as warning came into my mind. 'So, you look forward to some man's throbbing robin in you now.' I giggled again. I caressed it with an immaculately varnished nail, then took his scrotum into the palm of my hand and squeezed just enough so that he felt the power of me. The pre cum already oozed from him and I licked it ever so gently, feeling him shudder and he wrapped his fingers in my hair, I took him into my mouth, rhythmically sucking. I was rewarded by a moan of ecstasy and it took but a short time for him to come. He gathered me up in his arms and carried me to the bed lowering me gently and crouched astride me.

'May I look?' he asked.

'Of course mon cher,' I replied.

'It is marvellous, what they did for you in San Francisco. May we try?'

'I want you to. You are the first, I am your virgin.'

Slowly with my guidance, he lowered into me until we were as one, fully joined, his throbbing penis completely within me. I gasped with a little pain and then as that subsided, euphoria filled me.

'Do me, baise-moi cheri,' I whispered, 'baise-moi maintenant.'

'I see your French is improving,' he said, laughing at my coarseness.

Slowly he began to grind, occasionally moving left or right, bringing a gasp from my lips which then sought his. His tongue flicked out, parted my lips and flicked my tongue then gently his lips roved around mine, so gently that it tickled unbearably and I had to clamp my mouth to his for relief. He smiled down at me, laughing at my reactions. His left hand clamped across my right breast and he pulled at the nipple then sucked it. I thought I was going to die from the assault on my senses. Simon came first but after a gasp he continued until I came, my back arching, my senses exploding, diaphragm seeming to twist within me and we both subsided, still joined. We lay, kissing, caressing, I giggled and he smiled, kissing my face from brow to chin, leaving no surface unrewarded. His underneath hand held a breast, his other roved over my hip, buttocks and thigh. We smiled at each other and he gripped my head, pulling me close to his rough cheek, itself a thrill, the stubble like sandpaper against my skin.

We dozed, then I would feel for him, and reactivate the passion, or he would turn me and insert a finger, then as I came to, we made love again and again. Morning and parting came too soon. At seven he had to shower and I joined him there, then still nude, my hair still wet, he kissed me goodbye. Tears welled as I realised that we would not enjoy such a night together again for a long time.

He was gone. His aura lingered with me. I glowed within from the fire of his love and passion. The night of my virgin appearance as a fully equipped female had been wonderful. I returned to my apartment and collapsed into bed. At first I could not sleep, my thoughts and senses still aflame, but suddenly I was asleep. I awoke to find Sam there beside me.

She ruffled my dishevelled hair. 'So how was it? All you hoped for?'

'It was divine. He was a God. It was so much more than I expected, and I am so glad that he was the first. I just can't tell you how wonderful I feel.'

'And now he has gone. When will he be back?'

'I don't know. He is marrying Catherine Schûster. Oh yes we will see each other but I doubt we will be physical lovers. That is why I wanted to last night. He marries Catherine next week, un mariage de convenance. She bears his son and hopes to have two more before they part and we can be together.'

'That is a terrible burden for you.'

'I always knew it would not be conventional, but Simon has to have an heir, wants to have children, and that is something I cannot give him. I have to settle for what I can get, play the cards that life has dealt me and not wish for an ace when I only have a king. I remain a realist. Logic has got me this far and while I am as emotional as anyone, often more so, I remain a realist. That hopefully, eventually I will be with Simon, must be enough, and I will be here, in the background, family friend, protégé. Simon says that I am allowed to amuse myself meanwhile.'

'So, he has given permission? Is that his to give in the circumstances?'

'It is not like that. I am free, he says, to live life, enjoy my life like any other teen and twenty.'

Sam put her arms around me, and we kissed. 'I'm glad I have you as a friend. I admire you so much for the way you manage your difficult life.'

'You know me, Sam, Scarlet O'Hara. When things are difficult, I think about them tomorrow. Now let's get dressed and see the sights. Also I have to go to the Sorbonne and sign some entry forms. We'll have breakfast on the way, a cup of coffee and a bite like real Parisiennes.

Chapter 2.

We walked to Opera metro and took the number seven to the Louvre. We emerged into a sunlit day and found a cafe to have breakfast where they had fresh hot rolls rather than greasy croissants. Sam chose the latter and an orange juice while I had a yoghurt and café au lait.

We people watched while we talked, drinking in the atmosphere. We went down into the Metro again and onto the number one to Bastille, changing there to the number five for Saint Marcel.

L'Hôpitale Pitié-Salpêtrière was not what I expected when I saw it in August. I was looking for a great old building, probably Napoleon III, in classic French style, but instead, it was all very different. The Boulevard de L'Hôpital is very long and straight, with small shops built under quite modern apartment blocks. It was all disappointingly 1960s architecture, not romantic Paris. As we walked away from the Seine, we came to a sign on our left and the entrance. The building itself looked like another apartment block or rather an office block in sort of white stone and cream stair and lift sections. When I had come in a taxi, I did not take it all in but now I was so disappointed. This was modern ugly and I could have been in beautiful ancient Cambridge.

We entered the foyer and I announced that I was a new student and the receptionist, a dark haired woman with very red lipstick, gave me a little map and marked it with an X. Sam took the map and guided me. Eventually we came to the student office. I signed in and was given the Guide Pratique de l'Étudiant and some papers announcing that the welcome week was September 10th to 14th. Apparently older students in red tops conduct the students round the university, making sure their papers are all in order and that they have some knowledge of the geography and where they are supposed to be.

This meant that Sam and I had a week together. After that she would have to amuse herself during the day. It was all rather daunting, especially as I had difficulty making the receptionist understand me. I just hoped I was not making a huge mistake.

Sam did not mind the change in arrangements. We would be in contact by phone, so could keep up with texts. She wanted to do the sights, anyway, and I had already done many of them and also, she wanted to shop. So did I.

I needed some new student type gear so we decided to go and see what France had to offer. We wandered the streets ending in the Champs Élysées . We shopped there until we had exhausted the stores then made for Rue de Rivoli and Lafayette. We caught a taxi home laden with packages. Entering the apartment, I found a note from Madame Gameau, she had put food in the fridge.

We found cold chicken and a salad, just what we needed. After our dinner, we put on a dress show. I had gone for young smart and chic. Grunge was not for me. I wanted pretty and I think I achieved it with some primary colour mini skirts and smart tops, chiffon blouses, self support stockings in various shades and denier and scarves. Sam had gone for traditional student jeans and T shirts. Her one bright item was a pair of pink jeans with blue embroidery.

I went to bed with the university guide. As I read I realised that I had come to a place that was very unlike English universities. The course was five years minimum which I knew, followed by a minimum four years in house training before becoming a registrar. At the end of the first term there was a severe weeding out of students who did not reach the standard. At the end of the first year there was another weeding. By then eighty per cent would have fallen out. The work too was far more intense. Fun was not going to be what I was here for. The next four days then, we would fill with fun I hoped.

Next day we walked to La Madeleine and took breakfast, and strolled through the Tuileries, crossing the Seine at Pont Royale. I showed Sam where the Musée d'Orsay is as well as the Louvre and l'Orangerie. We travelled into the left bank and browsed the boutiques and people watched from a famous café. My new outfit attracted attention and when I watched myself in a shop window, I realised how strikingly different it was from the norm. It was not outrageous, just stylish and as we sat, a lady in her fifties at the next table who had been eyeing us turned and spoke.

'Excuse me, but you are the model, Trudi, isn't it?'

'No madame, not a model now. I am a student at the Sorbonne, studying to be a doctor.'

'But it is you, Trudi. I was at the show when you fell with that other girl. This is my card.'

The card said her name was Mlle Dufour, editor of Paris Mode.

'I wonder whether you would give me an interview, tell me about your life and why you are studying in Paris?'

'Mlle Dufour, I will think about it, but I have much to do at the moment, starting university next week and here with my friend who is on holiday. Perhaps I can phone you in two weeks?'

'You can't give me a half hour now?'

'No Madamoiselle, we have an appointment, I am sorry. I will phone you. Come Sam, we have to go,' I said pulling Sam to her feet.

'Au revoir Mlle,' I said to Madame Dufour. I would ask Simon about her before I made any interview.

We wandered the streets and boutiques till lunch, then made our way to Montmartre. As we sat for a citron on the pavement at a restaurant just below Sacré Coeur, Sam's phone rang. I could tell at once that it was bad news.

I reached across and held her spare hand. As she put the phone down, she blurted out, 'My father has had a stroke. I am sorry Trudi, but I have to go home.'

'OK, of course. If we hurry we can get you on a train this afternoon.' We left our glasses and found a taxi. In twenty minutes we were home. While Sam was packing I phoned Eurostar and managed to get, at an enormous price, a first class seat on the 16.43.

Having asked the taxi to wait, I made sure that Sam had all her goods packed and then we were on our way to Paris Nord. We just reached the station as the gates were closing and there was only time for a quick embrace and kisses. The tears flowed. I watched as she ran down the platform dragging her case behind her.

I took the Metro back to Opera. I entered my apartment alone for the first time. I sat for a long time looking out of the lounge window into the courtyard. Madame Gameau picked some herbs from her garden. I pulled up my knees to my chest and fell asleep.

My doorbell ringing awakened me. I straightened my mini skirt and ran fingers through my hair and opened the door expecting to see Madame Gameau. Eleanor stood there looking as though she had not slept for a month. Her desert trousers and boots and T shirt were filthy and she stank. She dragged a bag behind her.

'Where have you come from?' I asked in surprise.

'Mogadishu. It was awful. Can I have a bath Trudi. I feel I shall never be clean again.'

'Of course Ellie.' I took her to the spare room. I removed the towels Sam had used and replaced them from the airing cupboard, while the bath ran. I threw in some of my most expensive bath salts, and lit candles as she stripped. Nude she walked to the bath and climbed in, hardly looking at me.

I left the door ajar and collected up her dirty clothing, putting it and the towels in the washing machine. I managed to decipher what washing powder was from the packets in the kitchen and set the machine going. Next I stripped the bed Sam had left and as sheets were not to be found, I ran down to Madame Gameau. She soon arrived with fresh linen and insisted on making the bed herself. I said that I could do it, but she was adamant.

'Monsieur Le Comte has asked me to look after you. It is my duty. Non, you do not. Allez! Assistez à votre amie.'

I knocked the bathroom door and entered. Eleanor lay, just soaking. I was worried that she had fallen asleep.

'Are you OK. Can I do something?'

'I'm exhausted. I was lucky to get out.'

I picked up a sponge and soaped it then I took one arm and washed it, then the other and eventually her whole body until she was completely clean. There were bruises all over her arms and some on her back as though she had been very roughly handled. Her hands were unkempt, the nails broken. I fetched a file and set to work. At first she protested then gave in. I washed her hair with the shower and pulled the plug. Somehow I managed to coax her out of the bath and onto the stool. I dried her completely and dressed her in a robe. I took her to the bed and helped her in.

'Are you hungry?'

She shook her head. I dried her hair, combing out the tangles carefully until she said, 'No more, let me sleep.'

I left her. I found Madame Gameau in the kitchen, taking the washing from the machine and putting it in the drier. A tureen stood on a trivet. I lifted the lid. It smelled divine.

Alone, I ate some with fresh pain de compagne, delicious, leaving plenty for Ellie later.

Before I went to bed, I looked in on her. She slept as if dead, half prone, one leg brought up as though she was hurdling. I left her bedroom door ajar and mine too, so that I could hear if she roused. It was a long time before I got to sleep.

When I awoke, it was full daylight. I put on a negligee and went into Ellie. She was awake. She greeted me with a wan smile.

'It is so marvellous to be clean. Thank you for looking after me last night, you are such a darling. I felt just like a baby.'

'Do you feel better?'

'Much. And hungry. I haven't eaten anything but brown rice for a week.'

'What have you been doing?' I sat cross-legged on her bed. She still looked awful, drawn, so much older than a year ago when she had shared my bed for the last time.

'My job. I have been to the refugee camps, That was terrible enough. I was sick, literally, with the death and the smell. Then I was taken prisoner by some gang, I don't know who, there are so many different clans and sects. After three days, I managed to talk myself out of it, pretending that I was a nurse. I treated one man for a gunshot wound, extracted the bullet from his arm with a nail file, and used all my first aid stuff on him so as a thank you I found myself thrown into a pick-up truck and left at the airport. I was very lucky.'

'Oh Ellie. It is so dangerous. Can't you cover fashion or something? Peep behind the scene and see all those half dressed models?

'I like the danger, but it's not a bad idea. I like the thought of half dressed girls, rather than Kalashnikov carrying zealots.'

'I am full of admiration, but I hate to think of you in such danger.'

'It's what I like doing. I have been looking at your crutch.'

'I know you have Ellie.'

'So you are now complete as a woman?'

'Yes Ellie, at last.'

'I will have to check.'

'I'm going to get dressed, Ellie, so don't get excited. Then I'll get some breakfast. What would you like?'

'Anything other than brown rice.'

I showered and dressed in a mini eight inches above the knee and wide hemmed in French blue, and a see through top with a chemise underneath. Red hold-up stockings nearly reached to my skirt and black high heels completed the outfit.

I assembled all the good things I could find for breakfast, apples and nectarines, some nutty cornflakes. I fried some bacon and eggs, tomatoes and some hash browns from a packet in the freezer, things supplied by Madame Gameau which she thought were eaten by les Anglais.

Ellie drifted in, clad only in a T shirt and pants. 'Wow! This looks great.'

She started with cereal, then the bacon, eggs and tomatoes. When she had finished off with fruit, she produced a cigarette, a Gauloise. 'Do you mind?'

'Just this once Ellie, next time you have to go out on the veranda and close the door after you.'

'So, do I call you Comtesse?'

'Don't be silly, Ellie. Simon marries Catherine Schûster at the weekend.'

'Oh. I thought.......'

'You shouldn't think. Simon and I have a good understanding. He needs Catherine and I wish him well. Meanwhile I am here. He has done all this for me and I start at the Sorbonne next week. It is all so exciting, I haven't time for other things. I have to do well Ellie.'

'Of course. So you will be a doctor. Little Trudi. You have come a long way in what, just over two years. And look at you. A fashion plate in real life!'

'Is it too much? I don't want to be so, well, out there.'

'Not too much, just stylish. Young, vibrant. You look delicious.'

'What are you going to do Ellie?'

'How long am I asking to stay? Am I a nuisance?' she smiled.

'Not a nuisance. You can stay and recuperate, for as long as it takes. But you have to pay your way, and I am going to be busy and pre-occupied with starting uni. But I am pleased to see you, you know that.'

'Of course. Can I do my washing? I haven't one clean thing and these knickers of yours are a bit girly for me.'

'I think the clothes you pulled off last night are now clean. There might be something in my wardrobe. Let's see.'

I led her to my room and the walk-in wardrobe. 'Good lord. There is enough here for a princess let alone a Comtesse. I don't really think any of this is me. Too girly. But it is all very Trudi.'

Later when she had dressed in her fatigue pants and a T shirt, she came into the kitchen behind me. I felt her arms circle my waist, her hands across my stomach. Her face was in my hair.

'Gorgeous. You really are delectable Trudi darling.' A hand snaked up my skirt and into my pants. 'No little man. That is a shame.'

'No Ellie, it's wonderful. I am so happy now. I know who I am and where I am going. I have a wonderful benefactor, who I love and this wonderful apartment. Could life be better? This is the best yet, except that Simon has to be elsewhere.'

'So you love men? Have you done it, had sex with a man with your new anatomy?'

'Yes. It was marvellous, more than I ever thought. I am really happy Ellie, I mean really. Everyday, as I look in the mirror applying my make up, I just smile, seeing what I am and knowing what I was. It is more than signet and swan, much more. It is beast and beauty, the change colours my whole life and outlook. I am supremely happy. Even the daunting prospect of going to a foreign university seems an insignificant minor problem. I hated myself, now I love myself.'

'I believe you. I can see. Ma petite Trudi, my little love. And that outfit.............'

'So how about Ellie? Do you love yourself?'

'Of course I do. I am a good journalist. I wrote up my experiences on the plane and I should get a good fat fee from the paper. There might even be a book. I am well paid. I know who I am too Trudi. I love men, but I love women more, especially after the last few days. I love you more than ever in spite of no little man. It's intriguing. I would like to find out if you still react to me.....?'

'You are incorrigible.'

'Perhaps Simon would disown you if you slept with me?'

'Simon has placed no restrictions on me at all, in fact he actually mentioned you when he told me that he was to marry Catherine. It is a matter of whether I want to sleep with you. Whether I want a pervert in my bed, the older woman and the young girl.' I laughed. 'I really am not looking for sex with anyone Ellie.'

'No, but I felt, when I clasped my hands across your stomach, you liked it, I know you did.'

'What are we going to do with you? What are we going to do today? I think you should rest, you still don't look well.'

'I want to see life, be normal in a civilized society, that will make me feel better. I would like to have a wander in the Champs Élysées, then take cher Trudi, mon amie, for dinner on the Bateaux Mouches, s'il tu plait?'

'Wonderful, but the Bateaux, one needs to dress a bit. You will have to find something better to wear, and we will need to book.'

'You book. I will get myself organised. I need to wash more clothes too.'

'Mais oui, bien sûr.' (But yes, of course.)

We wandered to Le Champs and dodged into a few stores. Ellie emerged with some slacks, a shirt and a pair of medium heals, so she was equipped for dinner on the Bateaux Mouches. We sat on the pavement and people watched. I had adopted dark glasses to escape being spotted by another journalist, or anyone else. I told Ellie about Mlle Dufour yesterday and how we had to more or less run away.

'You're famous Trudi. As a journalist I would say that you are fair game for a story, but I can see your side. It might be good to give her a story and have it out in the open, then perhaps they will leave you alone.'

'What story? There is no story, I have not walked the catwalk for ages. I am now a student, trying to get an education in one of Europe's most famous fine cities. I am a private person and I also have to think of Simon. I do not want to damage him.'

'You are still a celebrity, and I think you always will be. Look how you are dressed. Do you see anyone else walking about here with so much individual style? Your dress is not odd, but it is unique. You could have just walked off the catwalk. If you do not want to be spotted then old jeans a floppy T shirt and dark glasses is the right way to go.'

'I want to keep my own style, chic chick, student. I am not into grunge Ellie, I leave that to you. Your mother never did grunge and she is my role model.'

'Of course you should do what you want to do, it is your right. I am just saying that it is almost impossible, certainly in this city, scene of your triumph and disaster, for you to escape attention. In any case, you are too beautiful.'

'Thank you, but really? I do not feel a beauty, I do not see a beauty when I look in the mirror, in fact I sometimes see a boy pretending to be a girl.'

'Have no fear, no one else sees that. Not Stuart, he still hankers for you, mother, well she sings your praises, thinks you are the most beautiful person in the world. Even Claire wants to be like you. I will give you my completely detached view. You should not compromise who you are, just because a few journos want to catch you out at a bad moment. You are so young, with so much potential. Enjoy every minute.'

We wandered down the avenue and arrived home early enough to have plenty of time to get ready. I ordered a taxi for the Pont d'Alma for 7.15.

I phoned Sam and found that she had arrived home to find her father had made good progress. He was still in hospital and would be for a few days yet. I was relieved. I resolved to send a card tomorrow.

I chose a dress Pierre had given me, the red silk with matching stiletto sling backs and a matching sequinned evening bag. I used straighteners on my hair and my smoky eye make-up. Even my nails matched the dress. For jewellery, I just wore the Swarovski bracelet I had purchased in Venice.

Ellie emerged from her room in the new blue slacks, light blue shirt and shoes she had bought that afternoon. She looked like a young man. She looked much better. Her face had relaxed, some of the furrows had gone from her brow. She had also plucked her eyebrows, and I thought I detected a touch of mascara. She still looked a dyke with her severe haircut, but a pretty one.

We were on board just before 7.30, the September sun dying in the west and the cloak of dusk descending over Paris on what had been another golden day.

Ellie announced that we were having the excellence menu and she was paying. We started with champagne, something we intended to continue as the evening went on.

I had chicken oysters, followed by fillet of beef. It was delicious. Ellie was great company, telling jokes and recounting some of her adventures around the globe. Just as I had done a lot in the last two years, so had she, on four continents, in war zones and disaster areas. She had seen war at first hand, babies dying of malnutrition, people buried under the wreckage of their homes. It made me all the more determined to be a doctor.

We had progressed to the cheese when a photographer appeared. I just heard the shout 'Trudi' and looked straight into the flash. It would not have been a good shot. Ellie called the fellow over. To my surprise, she convinced him to delete the shot in exchange for one posed. Better for them to have a good shot, she explained, than one that did not do me justice. I was coaxed out onto the bow, Notre Dame all lit up in the background and posed with my silk dress flying in the light evening breeze. Some passengers emerged to snap from behind him, most not really knowing who I was. Jules, the photographer asked what I was doing in Paris. I said that I was studying to be a doctor, but refused any other questions.

On the whole it was a lovely evening. I would be a liar if I denied liking the attention. I would have to speak to Simon and see what he thought. I am sufficiently vain to like being thought worth snapping.

It was nearly one a.m. when we entered the apartment. I removed my makeup and hung up the dress, then climbed into bed nude. I was almost asleep when I sensed a change. I found Ellie moving in beside me. Her arm was instantly about my waist, her hand across my abdomen, and I felt so weak at her touch.

'What are you doing? I asked foolishly.

'Exploring,' she replied.

'Not tonight Ellie, please.'

'I just want a cuddle. You do smell nice. Little Trudi, all grown up, my love. I will be good, promise.'

I fell asleep with her arm around me, the comforting feel of her hand across my stomach. In the night I think I rolled over and kissed her, but it could have been a dream.

When I awoke, it was fully light. Ellie was looking at me, her face one of amusement.

'Hello Ellie, good morning. Did you sleep well?'

'Oh yes, lovely. This is a really comfy bed. How are you?

'I'm fine, fighting fit. What are you going to do today?'

'We surely. Well first, can I look?'

'Why Ellie? I'm not an exhibit.'

'Because I love you.'

'You are all the most impertinent invasive person I know. No wonder you became a journalist. Leave me.....'

It was already too late, her head was under the sheet and she was pushing my legs apart. I could have resisted, but I might as well get the pestering out of the way. She threw back the sheet and knelt above me.

'From here one could not tell, even close, maybe.' Her fingers had already opened my lips and her skilled fingers were probing my vagina.

'You are all wet. I like that. I want to taste you,' and she dipped her head to my crutch and sampled me. 'Oh you are so sweet, like nectar. Some women have a bitter taste, but you, you are sweet from outside in.'

'Ellie, I take that as a compliment, I think. But I do not want to have sex with you.'

'Not sex darling, making love. I think you should experience a woman with your new anatomy, then you will know whether it is for you. Besides, I want to be the first.'

Suddenly her thumb was in me and another finger was in my anus, massaging, at the same time her lips plunged gently onto mine, and I knew I was lost to her. One hand below, the other playing with my breasts and it was the thoughts going through my head as much as what was being done to my body, that set me afire. I responded as Ellie knew I would, and then I thought, well, why not. If I enjoy what she does and I am denied Simon, then there is no reason not to. I orgasmed in no time at all, unable to hold back from this skilled assailant. Ellie giggled wickedly.

'I think you are a femme little dyke, my little Trudi. I just love saying your name. How did you get it? Did you choose it?'

'No, a friend, a neighbour's child, Heather. She was 18 months older than me. When they first dressed me as a girl, Heather chose the name.'

'So you were Tim, and they dressed you as a girl? Isn't that a strange unnatural thing to do?'

'Not really, given what I was like.'

'What were you like?'

'From my earliest memory, I hated being a boy. Instinctively I wanted girl clothes, toys, games, in other words I knew I was really a girl. What they did was supposed to deter me from my instincts, but it merely confirmed how I felt, what I already knew.'

'But if anyone had made me wear boy clothes, I don't think I would have wanted to be a boy'

'Ellie, that just goes to prove that I got what I wanted in the end, just by expressing my natural instincts.'

'Well, I am really grateful to Heather and whoever, for giving me Trudi.'

'I am not yours. I belong to me. Anything I do with you, or I allow you to do to me, is because I too want it. I like you Ellie and you amuse me, but if I had Simon, then I would not have you.'

'Ouch that has put me in my place.'

'Come Ellie, let's get up. We can stroll down to the Tuileries and have coffee.'

Chapter 3.

Over breakfast, I asked her what her plans were.

'Why?'

'Because I start my course at the Sorbonne, and I have to devote all my energies to that. You cannot distract me, and I won't let you.'

'You're very strong, aren't you? Not like you were a year ago.'

'I was a year younger and incomplete. I was quite in awe of you, and the family too. I was even frightened of Claire. I have done a lot since then. Grown up, become a woman. I have the power and support of dear Simon, rather than being as poor as a church mouse.'

'Are you asking me to go.'

'No, I am just setting some ground rules. You can stay, but you cannot disturb my studies, nor try to make me your plaything.'

'OK, OK, I get it. You are so harsh. Do you want to be here alone?'

'I don't know. I haven't been alone yet, ever, but I will have to get used to it. In some ways, I have been alone all my life, even when people are with me.'

'Hey Trudi darling! I know I seem superficial, but I do really know what goes on. You are right to remind me, because, well I look at you and I just see a woman and I love women but especially you. I treat you as I would any attractive woman who responds to me.'

'So where do you go next for work?'

'It depends what happens. If the agency want someone to go to a story wherever, I may be the one to go. In the meantime I write of my experiences and sell them where I can. However, I have my flat in London and there is the villa in Normandy and of course, my parents in Lincolnshire. I will stay to the weekend, if I may.'

'No, stay a bit longer. Simon marries Catherine on Saturday from the Château. I need some support. Please. I did not mean to be cross with you, it's only that sometimes, you make me feel like a plaything and I need a friend.'

'Come,' she said, taking my hand, 'let's explore the Left bank and look at the paintings. I feel your apartment needs something.'

We crossed to Quai d'Orsay and drifted along the river towards the Ile de la Cité and Notre Dame. We passed several stalls of paintings, all of Paris scenes, nothing special. Then we came to one of more abstract canvases, There were three with attractive colours, reds and blues, purple and gold. Ellie bought them all.

Next she propelled me into a jewellers. She selected a second hand ring, sapphire and diamonds. 'You haven't any rings, a pretty girl should have at least one.'

'No Ellie, it is too much.'

'It may be a long time before someone else buys a ring for you, so take it. Recompense for the way I have treated you and a sign of my love and respect.' She laughed. 'We will be engaged!'

I wore the ring, there and then and we wandered to the Tuileries again and home. I cooked steaks, onions and a red wine sauce and jacket potatoes, with green beans.

Each night after that, we shared my king size bed, but Ellie respected me. We cuddled and kissed only. Two days later I was at the Sorbonne for Welcome Week.

Chapter 4.

I was directed to the Atrium where we were divided into different teams, each with a red-coated senior as guide. Our group was about ten and I tried to keep up with the language and directions. They checked all our paperwork first then we were each given a pack of information. At coffee break a pretty dark haired girl named Élise sat with me.

'You are Trudi Nash, the Trudi Nash, isn't it?'

'Yes but I am just a student like you.'

'So really, you want to be a doctor when you could be a model?'

'That is why I am here. And you?'

'Of course, for me, I am not ugly but I am not beautiful, but for you it is different. You could have a great career as a model. You are already famous. Half the students have already recognised you.'

'I have long wanted to be un médicin. While I study, I hope to do a little modelling, to pay my way.'

'For La Maison Beauvonne?'

'Yes, I hope to.'

'Did you go to the wedding on Saturday?'

'No, I rarely see Le Comte. He is my benefactor, but his private life and mine do not often meet. I am just Trudi, trying to be the best I can. So where do you live, Élise?'

'In Gellainville, it is near Chartres, my father is a farmer.'

'Élise, I have a favour to ask? Would you help me through these first weeks, in case my French is not so good? Just keep an eye on me, please?'

'Of course, Trudi, c'est ma plaisir. It is time to go.'

Thereafter we were constant companions. Élise was quite a pretty girl, in spite of how she saw herself, curly dark coloured hair, darker than chestnut, over her shoulders with dark eyebrows. She wore the typical student dress loose T and a denim skirt and ballet shoes. I did stand out in my bright mini skirt and tops but I was setting my own style. I would not change to be one of the crowd.

All that induction week, we two stuck together, supporting each other. We came to know some of the others too, a small lad, Jean Luc, two girls who also stuck together, Simone and Julie, and three boys, Alexis, Giles and Vincent. The eight of us usually shared a table or sat about swapping notes. I soon felt quite at home. Élise filled the gaps in my

French and they all enjoyed correcting my grammar or teaching me colloquial French. It sounded nothing like the schoolgirl French I had been taught, I suppose something like estuary is to English. I had to know a few swear words. Merde, shit was used for everything and also the universal fuck. They taught me others, putain, whore or sometimes meaning fuck, me fait chier – that pisses me off, salope – bitch, con or connard – ass, casse toi – bugger off, and one they liked a lot, c'est vraiment des conneries – that really is bullshit. There were more usable phrases too. C'est le bordel – this is a mess, J'en ai-ras-le-bol – I'm fed up, peter des plombs, have a hissy fit. I decided to use them sparingly, but it amused them to teach English Trudi such things.

Ellie was usually at home when I returned. On Friday she met me with most of the gang at a bar just by the Louvre Metro. We shared three carafes of wine and some snacks. At eight we broke up, with multi kissing. Élise, Ellie and I went to the Opera to a good and inexpensive restaurant we had discovered. The three of us went to the apartment. As Ellie was still sharing my bed, Élise could have the spare room.

Élise came through as I prepared breakfast.

'How goes it?' I asked.

'I'm very good. I slept well. What a place you have here, I am so envious.'

'I am very lucky. Le Comte does not use this, so I am very lucky indeed, that he allows me to. So what is your plan for today?'

'I have to see my parents and tell them what my first week has been like. Non merci, pas de petit déjeuner. I must go. Trudi, I see you Monday, merci beaucoup.'

'I'll take you down, in case the door is still locked.'

We kissed in the doorway and she was gone. So one down and one to go. I was now longing to be on my own.

In the apartment, Ellie too had emerged. She caught me at the sink her arms once more circling my waist and her hands across my abdomen, making me feel so weak.

'What are your plans Ellie, only I now have work to do before Monday,' I lied.

'I am going tomorrow. See my parents, then back to work. I have booked the train, for 10.13, so can we be together today, then you have all day tomorrow?'

'OK, that will give me time. Thanks for your support while I settled in. It wasn't as daunting as I thought.'

'They seem a good bunch, your new friends.'

'They do. They have been teaching me very rude words, but I shall not use them. I want to remain well mannered, clean and studious, but fun. Élise says that I am a celebrity, so I have to be careful not to attract the wrong attention. I do not want to be notorious.'

'Perhaps you are already! Your history is known, so they will be waiting to pounce. I think you are right to be wary. Be careful with these new friends, they may not all be loyal.'

'I know. I will try to be, but I have to have some trust, or no friends.'

'You have survived so far, so.... Anyway, it is my last day. First I want to find a picture framer to frame those pictures, well two of them. I have Googled on my phone. There is one on Rue du Bac, across the Pont Royal. I feel lazy, we'll get a taxi.'

While Ellie was inside talking frames, I sat in the sun outside. It was so warm for September. I closed my eyes, just feeling the warmth, the buzz of traffic in the distance and

French voices near at hand. I was so contented. A kiss on my lips roused me.

'Done,' said Ellie, 'he will deliver to you. Let's find a nice spot to sit and watch the people go by.'

We found a café in a sheltered sunny spot out of the breeze and away from the rushing traffic near the university centre. As we sat with our café mochas I saw Jean Luc. I waived and he came to our table. He was a small young man, only five feet eight or so, swarthy, with oily dark hair, but a rather handsome fellow even so.

'I didn't think you would notice me Trudi. I waived when I saw you but you looked away.'

'I'm sorry. We were looking for a good table. Where do you live Jean Luc?'

'Here, over this shop,' he pointed to a small shop selling accessories, scarves in Eiffel Tower prints and other such trash.

'Join us.'

'I can't. I am working. This is my job, waiting table at the weekend to pay my way. I must ask what you would like Trudi?'

'Petit déjeuner si tu plait, Jean Luc.'

'Immédiatement.'

He disappeared into the cafe. The sun was really warm. Ellie was quiet, very quiet for her. My large sun specs hid me from her and everyone else and I felt quite secure.

'Are you OK, Ellie?'

'Yes, I am just thinking how I envy you. A student in Paris, all these young friends. I had a message from the Agency to go to Lebanon and try to get into Syria. I am not sure. I am going home first and will think about it. It is tempting because I will be seconded to the BBC, but it is also very dangerous. However it could lead to a BBC job, coveted in my world.'

The breakfast appeared supplied not by Jean Luc but another waiter.

We were drinking our third cup of coffee when Jean Luc appeared. This time he sat down.

'I have a break, so now I can talk to you. I need to tell you something Trudi. This year will be extremely hard for you. Many of this year's intake have already attended summer schools and studied one subject, so you are very behind. You must work extremely hard. Nearly forty per cent will drop out by October, because study in this first year is very difficult. The classes are too large and it is very competitive. At the end of the year, only twenty per cent will pass. If you fail, you can do first year just once more. It is extremely tough.

'I do not know whether you are really serious about this. The others think, as you are so well known, this is just a fun episode, that Trudi is a model playing at becoming un médicin. Is that it?'

'No Jean Luc. I want so much to be a doctor. I knew it was hard, but is it really that hard?'

'Yes. OK if you are really serious, then I will help. I am poor. My father is a ski instructor but in summer, he mends roads. I have to succeed. This first year is so competitive, students will try to make other students fail, so there is less competition. I cannot afford to fail or do a second year. Are you a clever girl or is there another reason you are here? How much do you want this? Be honest, don't mess me about.'

'Very much. Yes I am thought to be clever. This model thing has been fun, but that is all. I can work very hard.'

'OK. This is hard for me. I am going to fail, because I cannot work here and study. I am clever, but there is just not enough time. You need help, for a start you are English, your French is not so good yet. Medical French is strange to me and even worse for you. And these other students may seem friendly, but, they will cut your throat first, because you are not one of us, English and famous. They say, 'why does this English have to make our life more difficult?' Élise is not so bad. She tells me that you have a spare room. If I could stay with you, then we will have an alliance, I help you, you help me to study. We have three months till the first exam and if we fail we are out, only three months of really hard work before the exam, with no fun. But what one misses in class the other might get and we protect each other from dirty tricks. In June we have another exam. Do not make answer now. Think about it, then come and see me tomorrow with your answer. You can look on the internet, see what other people say. OK, back to work for me.'

'Merci Jean Luc. I'll see you tomorrow, here?'

'Oui.' He was already at a table taking an order.

'What do you think Ellie?'

'At first I thought he was looking for cheap lodgings, but you know, this all sounds very French to me. I said do not trust them. He has confirmed that, and if he depends on you, then he is hardly likely to stab you in the back. I like him. He is handsome in that dark French Mediterranean manner, and honest and hard working. As long as he has the spare room and your bed has room for me........'She laughed for the first time that morning.

'You are just too much Ellie. But I value your opinion. You are very perceptive. I have under estimated you, because you joke around so much, and always come on to me. Respect!'

'I need recreation from what I see when I work. Anyway, I will ring next time, before I descend on you. I hope you will let me stay.'

'I'm going to tell Jean Luc yes.'

I found him inside, serving cloth over his arm, waiting for an order. I wrote my address and phone numbers.

'Just come as soon as you like. My friend goes tomorrow early. So anytime will be good, even today.'

'Merci Trudi.'

Chapter 5.

Ellie had gone and I was alone in the apartment when the door bell rang. Madame Gameau stood there.

'There is a young man here,' she said, 'I don't know him.'

'C'est Jean Luc, mon ami de l'université, Madame. He is staying a few days to help me study. I come down.'

'So, does Le Comte know this?'

'He does not, but I will tell him as soon as he is available. At the moment he is away on his lune de miel, as you know, Madame Gameau.'

'This boy is not well bred, he has un accent de Savoie.' She puffed ahead of me into the lift.

Jean Luc stood looking sheepish with his few belongings waiting for us, Jerome by his side as if he were a thief.

I embraced him and led the way into the lift, leaving Madame and Jerome tutting behind.

'I am sorry for that Jean Luc. They are very protective of me and of course the house. It will be OK. I have to tell the Comte de Beauvonne, but he is away at the moment. Here let me help you. This is your room, and your bathroom here. Dump your things and come and see the rest of the apartment.'

Jean Luc followed mutely. 'I should not be here. This is not me. I'm sorry Trudi, but I do not want to make trouble. The concierge will tell the Comte and then we will both be thrown out.'

'No it will not happen. Let me make it clear now. This is two students helping each other, not un liaison d'amour, just so everything is clear. OK?'

'Of course. Trudi we can really work here. We will succeed. This afternoon I will show you all I have so far. I have a book list that we need, and as we are sharing it will be less expensive, but I have little money.'

'It is fine. Little rich girl will pay.'

That afternoon we spent sorting things out. We made a list of books, and I ordered them from Amazon on my account. Jean Luc showed me all his notes and outlined the different modules of the course and how the study went in France. It seemed like chaos. Luckily we were in the same class, amphitheatre three, stamped on our student cards, so we could sit next to each other. That would be a big help.

We ate some cold meats and whatever else we had, a bit of salad, then settled down and Jean Luc went through his notes in detail. Luckily I was good at molecular biology so that did not phase me, bio-chemistry was not too bad either by what I could see. I read through the excellent notes Jean Luc had made in the summer tutorials and we did a Q and A on them. We went to bed tired. The next day looked daunting.

If we were to survive the first three months we would need to work hard. The December exam would weed out many and with drop-outs in the first six weeks, the intake would be halved by the New Year. The system seemed deliberately difficult, programmed to fail most, so that a mere twenty percent would pass to second year.

It was not until three weeks later that Simon phoned to check on my welfare. I told him how difficult it was, and explained the system. He was surprised and apologised for having propelled me into such a competitive melée. He asked who Jean Luc was and I told him and explained our situation.

'Trudi, you do not have to explain to me. Madame Gameau was worried. I just want to know that you are safe and I want you to know that I care and I love you. The professor tells me that you are an excellent student, so I am very pleased.'

'How are you Simon? I miss you very much. When will I see you?'

'Before Christmas. Then New Year we go to Courchevel to ski. I would like very much for you to come. Bring your young friend, I would like to meet him, to give me peace of mind that you are safe.'

'That would be marvellous. Thank you. Jean Luc is really helping me. But for him, I would already have given up. I will ask him.'

All those autumn months we fought the system, scrounged the hand-outs, photographed the screens and recorded the lectures. At night we would eat an elementary meal, bought cooked chicken and vegetables mostly, then worked together until 10 pm. We sat the exam on 7th December and it was difficult. Somehow we both passed. The work recommenced.

On the 23rd December, Simon appeared in the evening, bearing several wrapped presents. I gave him my small gift, a pair of cuff links, said to have belonged to General de Gaulle, with the cross of Lorraine in gold on a white enamel background. I had bought them from a reputable dealer off Rue de Rivoli. We two went to dinner alone, Jean Luc having gone home to his parents in Bourg St Maurice for Christmas. Catherine was at home in the Château, now seven months pregnant. Simon spoke kindly of her, saying that she was well and having a good pregnancy. Oh yes, and she was having twins.

'That's marvellous news,' I said, 'congratulations Simon. I am so glad for you.'

We dined at Le Meurice on Rue de Rivoli. I had pigeon as a main, but I can't remember what else. I was all in a dither, my heart fluttering and my words twisted, being with Simon alone again. I managed to tell him about the course and how difficult it had been and how the next six months would be just as hard. I spoke about Jean Luc, and the help he had been and how we helped each other. I was breathless and a little shy, as though this was our first meeting.

We returned to the villa and I asked him to come to the apartment, to be with me.

'I want to, but I cannot.'

'I want you. I want to sleep with you.'

'No Trudi. Not here, not tonight. When you come to the Chalet Montagne in Courchevel, we will be together if that is what you want. Just remember that I do love you.'

'Why not tonight?'

'Because I am leaving now, to go back to the Château for Christmas with Catherine as I have to. On 27th I go to the Chalet. You will come on the 28th?'

'Bien sûr.'

'Good. And Jean Luc?'

'Yes. He is a good skier, his father is an instructeur de skier.

'And you will sleep with me then?'

'Bien sûr, of course

'Joyeux Noel, mon cher Trudi.'

We kissed and then he was gone, leaving me alone in the apartment. I went to bed with a sigh. This moment was the lowest point in my life, since emerging from my male life at school. My first Christmas and I was alone.

I awoke on what in England is Christmas Eve, dull of mind. Listlessly, I went about tidying the apartment, shoved washing in the machine. I stripped Jean Luc's bed and his bed clothes followed mine. Then I remade both our beds. It was nearly eleven.

The knock at the door startled me. Opening it I expected to find Madame Gameau. Instead I found Simon.

'What are you doing here?' I asked.

'May I come in?'

'Of course. I thought you had gone to the Château? Why are you here?'

'Catherine asked where you are, and made me return to collect you to share our Christmas. You can do that?'

'I don't know. It might be too difficult to pretend. Could you not have telephoned me.'

'Catherine said that you would refuse if I phoned. She made me come in person. So here I am.'

'I still don't understand. Why is Catherine concerned for me?'

'She knows that you are my protégée. She asked where you are and what you are doing. She insisted that you cannot be here alone at such a time. She wants to meet you.'

'I don't think so. I mean it is too much. I would have to live a lie, tell her lies.'

'If you do not come, she will be very puzzled. Of course she knows that I am very fond of you.'

'But not how much and in which way?'

'Look, you know that our marriage is one of convenience. Catherine knows that. We will not be like lovers with her. We don't do that, but here in France, we have such arrangements. Really it is OK. Then we go to Courchevel together for four days, while Catherine stays home. She does not want to risk falling and hurting the babies. So pack now quickly, I help you.'

'I have no ski clothes!'

'We buy in Courchevel.'

I packed and we were soon in his Mercedes speeding out of Paris. This ride was a highlight of my life so far. There is nothing so intimate, apart from sleeping, as a couple together in a motor car. I rested my hand on his thigh and he on mine. The sensation was electric. The ride was like a dream. We passed Chartres then turned North West towards Alençon. I was surprised how soon we arrived at the Château. It was huge, I had forgotten how large, with no moat, but a broad gravel path ran right around it. We swung into the wide gravel area and left the car beside the front door. My stomach had turned to butterflies and gurgled.

'Courage Trudi, it's OK.

My bags were carried in by Michel, who was butler come chauffeur. Catherine met us in the salon. I had seen her photo in Paris Match, so I knew that she was an imposing woman. About five feet nine inches in her stockinged feet, long dark hair flowing over her shoulders and slim, she certainly was a head turner. She had abandoned the lap top she was using and came forward to greet us. They kissed, and she turned her attention to me. Her eyes seemed to pierce my skin and examine my soul. I do not know when anyone looked at me so minutely. I looked directly into her smiling face and detected amusement in her smile.

We shook hands and kissed. 'Simon, is Trudi's room ready? Go and make sure while we get to know each other. So Trudi, how are you and how is the university course?'

As I started to reply, Simon left presumably to make sure my room was ready. Darkness had descended and Catherine pulled the last of the huge curtains.

'The course is very hard, but so far so good.'

'And you, you are well?'

'Oui, Comtesse, merci.'

'No, you call me Catherine. Do not be shy or formal with us, we know all about you. As Simon's wife and his PR consultant, it is my duty to know everything. I love Simon, though he does not love me so much. But I now have a position in society through our marriage. I would not like to see my life disturbed, nor Simon's reputation damaged. You wouldn't like that either, would you?'

I shook my head dumbly. I realised that she was setting out the rules, letting me know how far and where I could go.

'You are not yet nineteen. It pleases Simon to help you, so that is how it must be. You will continue to live in the apartment and finish your studies. By that time, Simon will have come to his senses and you will probably have found some other little pervert to be with. You will leave us alone. If Simon wants a little fling with you, now and again, then that will be fine. At least with you, there will not be any little bastards.

'So my dear Trudi, I should go up. Freshen up and change into a nice robe, then come down to dinner. I would rather you did not hurt Simon by repeating this conversation. You see he is settled with me now.'

I turned with tears in my eyes. Now I knew why Catherine had insisted Simon brought me here. As I entered the vestibule, Simon was near the bottom of the stairs. I blew my nose, to disguise the hurt.

'Ah Trudi, come I show you your room.' He held out his hand to take mine, but I could not take it.

The room he showed me into was enormous, too large, I felt lost in it. Everything was gold and blue, like a palace. The en suite was superb, filled with perfumes and bath salts. On the bed my outfit for the evening was left out. Shoes, stockings and a black dress, mourning for my childish dreams of being his love, his wife I thought. The death of all my day dreams, of riding with him over the estate, of being on his arm at important receptions and functions. Catherine had passed judgement on me and destroyed me.

I stripped and made my way into the bathroom. I sprinkled Channel into the bath and ran the taps. I lay a long time in the bath, thinking what to do. When my skin started to wrinkle, I pulled the plug. I resolved to be the best I could possibly be, better than Catherine in every way.

I moisturised my skin, then blow-dried and straightened my hair. I made my face with great care. There was no time to do my nails other than with a quick manicure and a coat of semi transparent pearl varnish. The dress was from House of Beauvonne, beautiful jet black silk, strapless, revealing my straight back and an amount of cleavage. It contrasted with my pale Nordic skin. I surveyed the result in the full-length mirrors of the Empire wardrobes, checking carefully to make sure that every part of me was perfection. I took my best jewellery from the box and adorned my wrist and neck. I wore the ring given me by Ellie on the third finger of my left hand, like an engagement ring.

I descended the staircase, careful to keep my head up and careful not to trip or fall, a smile upon my face. The vestibule was full of people. I had not realised that this was to be anything else than a dîner de famille.

As I descended, faces turned to watch and Simon detached himself from Catherine and three other people to reach out his hand to support me as I reached the last step. I smiled my thanks, giving as good a representation of happiness as I could manage. I kissed him on the cheek. He introduced me to several people, local landowners, a distant cousin. I remembered a couple of names. I sipped my glass of champagne and chatted to two ladies who wanted to know all about my modelling.

'I have little knowledge about that Mesdames,' I said. 'I am a student at the Sorbonne, studying to be un médicin.'

They expressed surprise. 'It is what I want to do, to help people.'

'But le Comte said that you were a model now.'

'If I have the time and it does not interfere with my studies, then I will pay for my keep. But this first year is very difficult and we study day and night or fail. Next year it may be possible, I have to see.'

A dark haired girl with bushy brows but a nice face, slightly familiar, spoke to me.

'You don't remember me, Trudi la modèle?'

'No, I'm sorry.'

'Sabine, the groom when all your friends went riding. You did not ride. Can you not?'

'I do remember now, Sabine. I don't think we were introduced. How do you do?'

'Wow, so formal, Trudi. Come over here, I want to say something.' She led the way to a deserted part of the room. 'I don't know you Trudi, only of you. How old are you?'

'Eighteen.'

'I am twenty-four, with a degree in Agriculture, but that does not matter. Here I am a groom. I just want to say, look out. La Comtesse is like the Queen in Snow White, and she does not like you. That is all, Trudi la modèle.'

'Thank you Sabine, I already know. Don't call me la modèle please. I don't like it.'

'But isn't that what you are famous for?'

'Oh yes, but my friends do not address me in that sarcastic manner, and I would quite like to be your friend. Why do you stay here if you don't like it?'

'Simon is my uncle, well sort of, and round here there is no other work for me. I like horses and I am a good horsewoman. I wish you no harm. I thought you were not a serious person, a bimbo. I see I was mistaken. Just be careful. Don't put too much trust in either of them. I say no more.' She turned on her heel and left me as a ginger haired man approached.

She reminded me of the resistance leader in that TV series, 'Allo Allo".

The newcomer introduced himself. 'I am Gérard, I'm taking you into dinner, Trudi.' He offered his arm and we followed others into the dining room. He was just under six feet tall, so that in my six inch heels I was nearly three inches taller.

The party numbered twenty-four, small enough for everyone to know everyone else. Simon sat at the head and Catherine at the bottom of the table. I found my place was to Simon's left and on my left was Gérard. Opposite me were a couple who I had been introduced to as Monsieur and Madame Picot, an industrialist from Le Havre. Picot was as attentive as Gérard, asking after my health and enquiring after my studies. Sabine was way down the table on the opposite side.

This was they told me, the traditional French Christmas, the gathering of friends and family on what in England we call Christmas Eve.

Simon was for some time engaged with Madame Picot, talking fashion trends and I heard my name mentioned but I could not hear the conversation because Picot and Gérard kept up a constant banter with me, teasing and joking. Simon did not speak to me until the third dish was served, telling me that it was lobster thermidor and describing the sauce.

I could feel Catherine's eyes upon us and making an adjustment to my napkin, I managed a glance to my left to see her. Her companions were speaking but she seemed inattentive to them.

'Are you OK Trudi?' Simon asked.

'Yes, my napkin was escaping. I have it. Simon I am a little worried about skiing. I don't know how to you know, so I would not want to be a burden. Perhaps I should give it a miss.'

'I have arranged a teacher for you, full time and you will be skiing after four days. I promise. No it is all planned. Don't be frightened.'

'Well it is partly fear, but also, I do not want to be the odd one, can't ski, doesn't fit in.'

'Oh you will no be left out. Truly it is all arranged.'

'Ah, so you *are* going to ski,' Gérard said, 'I am sure you will enjoy it. The cleanliness, the good air and sunshine and excitement, you will enjoy, I know. Does Catherine go to?'

'I asked her to, but she has declined because of any risk to the baby.' Simon replied.

'It is a pity, I so wanted her to come,' I said, 'I am just getting to know her. Simon is very lucky to have found her.'

'And do you have a boy friend Mlle Trudi?' asked Madame Picot.

'No Madame Picot, but I live with a boy. His name is Jean Luc and he is also a student médicin. We help each other study but it is purely platonic.'

At last the main dish arrived, roast turkey and another different wine, the third one. Then three sweets and another wine, followed by coffee and liqueurs. At last the meal came to an end. I was a little tipsy from all the wine. I rose to my feet before I had even thought what I was doing. I raised a glass and said, 'I propose a toast, to Catherine and two new Beauvonnes.'

I was surprised when they readily responded. Simon whispered 'thank you' to me.

Catherine responded too with a toast to Trudi and her studies. I mouthed thank you to her. Then excused myself for the toilet. I was sick. I drank water from the tap and was sick again. Having emptied my stomach I felt better. I cleaned up, and went to my room. I made my face again and returned to the drawing room, where I sat with Madame Picot and Mademoiselle Annette Sabourin. Annette was a beautiful thirty year old, her auburn hair bobbed, and lipstick bright red and perfect.

'I am pleased to meet you Trudi. Ever since you made the headlines two years ago, I have longed to meet you in person. You remember when you gave that press conference in Venice? I was there. I was very impressed that you took command of the situation. You were what, seventeen nearly? It was a magnificent performance. I work for ,' she mentioned a famous gossip magazine, 'so if you need help or want to give a story, then call on me.'

'Thank you. I was sixteen. Do you know a Madame Dufour?'

'Oh yes, I know her. Be careful. She has friends near at hand. Madame Picot, would you excuse us while we talk some business? Trudi, perhaps you would like to show me your room?'

I concurred, not quite knowing why. 'You go, make some excuse, perhaps petit mal oui and wait at the top of the stairs and I will follow in a few minutes. This is important for you.'

I spoke to Simon, pleading petit mal or a headache, said good night to the company, bobbed a minute curtsy to Catherine and left the room. I sat on the top stair waiting for Annette to appear. After five minutes the door opened and I saw her climbing the staircase. I led the way to my room.

Safely inside with the door closed, Annette sat on the bed with me.

'Firstly Trudi, you are more beautiful now than when I last saw you in Venice. I congratulate you on what you are achieving, and if I may say so, the way you conduct yourself. The toast to Catherine was inspired. No, don't deny anything. I know Catherine well, you see we worked together in journalism before she became a PR guru. She was an untrustworthy cat then and is now. She and I spoke earlier. She does not like you, but you probably know that. Of course Simon will not know that, it would break his heart. He is a good man, but perhaps too good. She told me tonight that she wants to dispose of you, create some scandal so that Simon will lose interest in you. So be very careful. I am in the ski party so I shall see you in Courchevel too and we can talk more.'

'She called me a pervert tonight. She also said that at least I could not bear any bastards. Annette, that really hurt. Yes you are right, that is why I made the toast to her, I was being ironic.'

'There are things in her past. I will make some enquiries. Perhaps I can give you some information which will keep her in her place.'

'Simon married her, believing that it was un mariage de convenance. He wants children, heirs to his estate but has said that he wants to marry me later, when my study is over and when the heirs have been supplied. He thinks she is committed to this plan, but she has reneged on the deal. I do not feel worthy of him, but I do love him. The plan seems to me just a dream now.'

'I will make a few calls, talk to people in the business about Madame la Comtesse. I know there is scandal. It will be a weapon, an insurance policy to make sure she does not hurt you.'

There was a knock at the door. I looked at Annette. She raised her eyebrows. Then said loudly, clamping her palm across my forehead, 'Come in!'

Catherine entered. 'Good, Catherine, I am glad you have come. Trudi has been sick and I helped her back to her room. Perhaps you have something? I think the rich food and too much wine for a young woman unused to such rich living.'

'Of course. I will get something.' She departed.

'Don't take it Trudi, you never know!' She laughed. 'Be very careful, she is a good actress but poison. Poor Simon.'

Catherine returned to find Annette pretending to take my pulse. She gave me two tablets that I took into the en suite and pretended to take.

'I will say good night then Mesdames. Thank you for looking after me.'

Annette made me turn and unzipped my dress, while I held it up around my breasts. They departed and I let the dress fall to the floor. I looked at myself in the mirrors. Pert breasts with rose areolas, trim waist, my black lace string and black hold-ups with lace tops. My legs are long and slim and look even longer in black court shoes. The sight pleased me. I am as I want to be, ultra feminine and at least good-looking even though others say I am beautiful. No one is going to take this away from me, certainly not Catherine Schûster, of that I am sure. At the same time, I want Simon to have the heirs he deserves.

I removed my make-up, slipped into my best nightdress and was just going to get into bed, when on impulse, I went over and locked my door. It was silly, I know, but suddenly I was frightened of Catherine and I wanted to sleep soundly. I remembered Jane Eyre.

Chapter 6.

When I awoke, it was daylight. It peeped from around the huge drapes and I could see that we had snow overnight. I slipped from my warm covers and drew the curtains back to reveal the parkland covered in a thin layer of snow. I felt rather the worse for wear. My sickness the previous night had emptied my stomach but the poison was still circulating in my system. I ran my bath and chewed on two stomach tablets as I soaked. I lay for a long time, wondering about Schûster, hoping that Annette Sabourin was genuine. I did not need this complication and intrigue.

I did my hair and face. I chose a heavy white silk shirt and grey slacks to wear with a three quarter length wool jacket. It was a warm and practical outfit.

In the salon I found Annette. 'How are you today?' she asked.

'I'm OK. No wine today though. And I think I will skip breakfast.'

'Perhaps a short walk. Have you boots against the snow?'

'Yes, as long as there is no snowdrift. I'll find a coat. See you in the vestibule.'

We met at the front door. Outside it was cold but not bitingly so. It was a windless day, the sun already lifting the cold and melting the light covering of snow. We strolled around the Château and down to the small lake. When we were way out of earshot and view, Annette spoke seriously.

'Catherine can be a dangerous enemy. She knows everyone and has power, because she knows so many secrets. So be very careful. About two years ago, just before she became the Beauvonne PR guru after the press tried to tie Simon as your lover, Catherine was living with her junior assistant, ç Clement. There was wide gossip that this was a lesbian relationship, because Françoise had appeared from nowhere, with no money or connections but was set up in a very classy apartment on Avenue Foch. When Simon employed Catherine, Françoise disappeared, left Paris apparently and has never been seen again. I think I know someone that knew her well and may have kept in contact. I will dig.'

'Why do you want to do this?'

'Because I do not like a bully and I have an affection for Simon. We are very old friends. No one was more disappointed than me when he announced the engagement to Catherine Schûster. Chalk and cheese, a woman I disliked marrying a man I liked a lot. But also, I admire and like you too, brave, intelligent and beautiful. A pity for you, that your body did not match your psyche, and yes, I know what happened to Simon's transsexual sister.'

'The last thing I want to do, is upset Simon by rubbishing his wife. I know the marriage is supposed to be a convenience, but it is his plan to have children, heirs, before we are together.'

'Ah Trudi. I see that you are truly in love. There is something you must always remember, that you love and respect yourself first, otherwise people will use you. The minute a relationship becomes one sided, with one person giving and the other taking, then you have to leave it. Are you going to live in the background of this marriage for the next seven years and be available for Simon when he feels he needs you? You are now a young woman, with I presume, sexual appetites. Are you going to live like a nun waiting on Simon's beck and call? Non, this is not the way.'

'Simon has not placed a restriction on me. He says I must do what I want to do. I live with a young student, although it is platonic. Jean Luc has not made any advances and at the moment, the university course is taking all our energy.'

'Fadaises, stuff. Two young people and you have no time for l'amour? Are you both sexless?'

'I do not want to complicate things with Jean Luc, or to offend Simon by having a live in lover.'

'Already you have played into Simon's hands. No he probably does not mean to limit you, but the promise of a future with him, living here, he has bought you, all tied up in a nice ribbon. It is a terrible situation. If he really loves you, then he will allow you to do all the things a young student will do, get drunk, get laid, dance till dawn, flirt. If he really loves you, he may become jealous. That is not necessarily a bad thing. It will keep him on his toes, or make him decide between you. But it is your life...' She shook me, looking deep into my eyes.

'Merci Annette. You have certainly made me think. I owe Simon a lot, but not my soul. I have only made love to a man once as a woman, and that was Simon.'

We had progressed into the shade of the lakeside forest, yet within me there burned a new fire of determination, to be as I wanted to be. I had not gone through my change, all the jibes and fun poking, the press intrusion to be a recluse, waiting forever for something that might never occur. Yes, I would behave with dignity, but I had assumed the role of a woman and as a young female student in the fine city of Paris, I would behave like one.

We made our way back to the Château under the eyes of Catherine who stood at the window. I went to my room and took out my study books, looking at the curriculum for the next six months. I remained engrossed until the light faded with the falling dusk. No one had disturbed me. It was a relief. I had just put away my books when there was a knock at the door. Opening it, I found Simon there.

'I was worried about you Trudi. No one had seen you since this morning and you were unwell I think last night.'

'I am fine. Yes a little unwell last night, so much food and wine. I am not used to the richness. I have been studying.'

'Have you opened your presents?'

'I had forgotten them Simon.'

'Then I will take them down and before dinner we will open them as is our custom here.' He gathered the half dozen boxes. 'Make yourself beautiful, yes?'

'Ah oui, Monsieur Le Comte. C'est ma plaisir.' Simon looked at me quizzically, then laughed and departed.

I spent a long time on my hair, making sure it was straight and shining. It glowed like molten gold, and flowed over my shoulders like silk. I held back on the makeup, settling for defining and shading. My eyes looked like deep pools. I wore my favourite red dress. I descended deliberately five minutes late, to make an entrance and to annoy Catherine. Simon put out an arm and circled my shoulders with it, like a fond uncle.

'Here she is. Now we can begin.' Simon said, Catherine watching like a snake its prey.

He became the present giver, selecting them from different piles, first Catherine who received a fine modern diamond necklace. Then Annette, some kid gloves and Hermes scarves.

Simon presented me with a large box. Inside was a most beautiful light tan leather jacket, peplum style with a high collar and ornate quilted front. Underneath was a pair of jeans from Givenchy, with pretty embroidery on the upper right leg. I rose and kissed him.

He chucked me under the chin. 'There might be more,' he said.

Then it was Gérard. Simon gave him a large heavy parcel. He tore at the ribbon and the wrapping, inside was a polished wooden box. He snapped back the catches and revealed a shot gun.

'Mon chèr cousine, this is magnificent. I am so glad I came.' He laughed, broke the gun and checked the barrels in the light, then snapped it shut and put it to his shoulder, 'Boom, boom.' He shouted, then leant the weapon against his seat and grasped Simon kissing him on both cheeks.

Catherine received a fur coat next, a beautiful dense dark mink. I hoped not to receive the same. I was not disappointed. A jewellery box in red leather, revealed a diamond bracelet with matching ear pendants. It was a wonderful generous gift from Simon. So the giving went on. Simon opened my gift of the cuff links and read the history, that these were the ones de Gaulle had worn every day while in London during the war, and which he had given to his chef after D Day. He was enchanted.

I had no present for Catherine, nor she for me. We sat on opposite sides of the salon, making piles of presents. The five of us then went in to dinner, a mere three courses. I had one glass of wine and made it last with more glasses of water. Catherine did not speak to me directly, but once said during a discussion on French politics, 'I wonder what Trudi thinks?'

'I am not French Catherine, so I do not have any preformed ideas. I see some good in the Socialists but also in the neo-Gaullists. What I most admire in France, is that the people value their democracy, while many British people do not care a jot. French people had a terrible struggle to get democracy while we rather fell into it. My experience of the University confirms my view, that anyone can enter the course, but they are then weeded out on performance, while in Britain you cannot start the course unless you already have the required qualifications. In France it is hard, but more democratic.'

'A very long speech from a young woman who professes to know nothing.' Annette said.

'Yes,' said Gérard. 'A very good answer, I think. Caught you out there Catherine.'

'Perhaps Trudi would like to be French,' Annette smiled, 'would you.'

'I am already English. That is my birth-right. Britain has a long and honourable history. I am proud of my nation. However, I recognise that not everything is perfect there, nor here. If I could be both French and British, that would be good. In the meantime I am une Européenne.'

Gérard kissed my cheek. 'Bravo chère Trudi.'

By the time I went to bed I was very tired. I locked my door again, foolishly thinking of the queen in Snow White. I placed my lovely presents on a chair where I could see them. I was so lucky. My life was like a fairy tale. My dreams were disturbed by a dark haired queen offering a golden apple. I awoke, punched my pillows and subsided into a deeper sleep.

The next day, I had breakfast, and returned to my room to study. At midday, Simon knocked my door to take me down to a light lunch of pigeon breasts and salad. Afterwards it was back to my books, staying clear of Catherine. Dinner passed off OK, Catherine had obviously divined the mood of the others who supported a jeune fille, and left me alone. I could not wait to be out of the Château and off to the fairy land of Courchevel.

Chapter 7.

Next day we were up early, Simon and I, Gérard and Annette in separate cars set off to Courchevel. I wanted to say goodbye to Catherine, but Simon said she was not yet up, but that she would understand.

We drove in convoy, south to Tours then to Clermont Ferrand. It was to be a nine hour drive, so we should arrive by six, allowing two hours for lunch. I was glad to leave Catherine behind. It was cosy in the car, just Simon and I. Sometimes Gérard and Annette would be in front, sometimes us, Simon's Mercedes and Gérard's BMW heading nearly all the way across France. We stopped for fuel and a light lunch in Thiers. Another three hours and we were into the Alps. We cruised into Moutier just on five, and began the long climb up the zigzag to Courchevel. As we climbed the temperature dropped and the snow cover gradually increased. We passed through the different villages built for skiing, Courchevel1500, 1650 and eventually reached 1850. We left the cars in the underground car park. We were met by Simon's chef, Robert, and his wife with two skidoos. Our luggage was placed on towed sledges, and they zoomed off uphill into the darkness. We took the Jardin Alpin bubble lift. We exited and took a short walk to a traditional looking chalet, log built with huge overhanging roof and carved balconies, one of the originals, situated amongst pine trees. Wood smoke filled our nostrils, a rare scent in most places. It was strangely comforting. We entered via a ski room, and the heat enveloped us immediately

We climbed stairs to emerge into an open plan lounge diner, a huge room some ten or 12 metres square. At one end was a ground to floor window and in the half-light one could still see down to the centre with the various ski lifts radiating from it, and beyond, the twinkling lights of the valley. Simon led the way up another staircase to a landing with several doors off. He opened one and ushered me in. Inside was a large bedroom with an en suite off. The bed was ornate and king-size. Simon grasped my arm and propelled me towards it. As I looked back startled, he picked me up and planted me on the bed, and expertly divested me of my clothing until I lay in just brassiere and panties. I was relieved that I had worn a new set in pink silk and fine lace. Simon stood back, surveying my almost nude body. If I had still been a boy, I would have hated that. Now in my female form, I was not shy at all. It all seemed so right.

'I am going to fuck you now, Trudi. I hope you are ready for this. All over Noel, I could not stop thinking about you.'

He peeled off his clothes, carelessly throwing them to the floor after mine, until he stood completely nude in the subdued lighting. Nervously I fingered myself, making sure that I was wet. Just in case I shot off the bed, collecting my handbag as I ran to the bathroom. I filled myself with KY. I was glad that I had taken the time to go to the beautician and had my pubic hairs waxed to a minimal shape. I was tempted to have them permanently removed, perhaps I would. Unafraid and unashamed, I re-entered the bedroom. I was immediately seized from behind, a hand pushing between my legs, his hand cupping my mound of Venus and a shudder went through my body and a moan escaped my lips. He propelled me onto the bed, turned me, spreading my legs wide and pushing my knees towards my breasts.

He eased me apart and inserted his index finger, massaging, pushing seeming to stretch me inside. He crouched above, fondling my breast with his spare hand, pinched my nipple, and both nipples immediately expanded.

'Suck me first, like you did in September. I have been dreaming of that night ever since.'

I thought back to that fateful day, when Mother had taken me up the road to Heather's house and they had dressed me in Heather's cast off clothing. My brother had called me a cocksucker. And so I was, and I didn't care. It seemed so right with this lovely man.

I took hold of his penis, gripped it and squeezed as though milking a cow. I pulled him over and onto his back and swallowed him. I withdrew, scraping my teeth across his skin, making him gasp and writhe, his hand now entwined in my hair. Slowly I began to suck him, my tongue playing with the head, a slow rhythm, sometimes stopping completely, so that he begged me to recommence. When he tried to finger me, I smacked his thigh hard and bit his penis enough to make him gasp. After that he soon came, his body jerking upward, trying to sink himself deep into my throat. I sucked him dry, savouring his sweetness. He asked me to suck again. Instead, I launched myself on top of him, guiding him into me. I rode him hard until he bucked and begged me to stop. I slowed, leaving seconds between each stroke until he begged me to restart. I rode him hard, we galloped to a finish, climaxing almost together. He cried out with the ecstatic pain. I lay, on his chest, keeping him within me, kissing him, nibbling his ears until he shivered. At length we rose and showered together, soaping each other intimately. We moisturised and I did my hair and makeup. I dressed in a tiered black silk skirt and a white silk shirt. I wore my new bracelet and ear pendants. We descended just before eight and found Annette and Gerard already there, watching television.

Robert informed us that dinner was ready. We started with baked spider crab, a Basque recipe I was informed, on a bed of salad, very rich crabmeat with cream, parsley and sherry. This was followed by magret of duck, oh so my favourite, in a rich plum sauce. The sweet was a delicious sorbet, followed by a cheese board.

We sat afterwards and they swapped ski stories. In the morning, Simon said, he would get me kitted out. We soon went to bed where we fell asleep quite quickly. I woke at 3 am. I felt his penis, large and semi erect poking into my buttocks. I grasped it and he came alive. I guided him into me. 'Baise moi, Simon, do me good.' He turned us and came on top.

I came first, the pain ripping up through my abdomen, so that I clenched him trying to stop the ecstatic pain that was too much to bear, but he would not until he also came and he subsided. I made him stay within me, loving the feel of him there and we once more fell asleep. Somehow we parted in the night and awoke to a dawn light behind the heavy curtains.

After breakfast, Simon took me in the bubble to the centre. We turned right out of the lift station and went into a ski shop on the right of the nursery slope. In no time I was kitted out in base and mid layers, salopettes and jacket, in a silky material, with studs and embroidery. They seemed a dreadful price, but Simon said I must have the best. The helmet cost as much as the jacket, a shiny black model with ornate silver work on it. The boots were huge and heavy and I wondered how I would ever walk in them. We hired skis, the best they had for a beginner. We returned to the chalet to find my tutor, a young blonde girl who I was surprised to find was English, Liz.

We were soon on the slopes, and I was unsteadily making my way down a green run, while Liz shouted at me. It was both thrilling and terrifying, but the second time I loved it. When I had mastered going straight and stopping we started doing some turns. I found it incredibly difficult but by lunch I was quite pleased with myself. Liz said I had done really well. The afternoon was hard. She made me do exercises, repeating motions over and over until I had grasped them. Above all she taught me how to stop, quickly, without hanging on to someone else or a tree, with a change of weight and a little hip swing.

Every night, Simon and I. made love as soon as dinner was over. On the third night, Gérard and Annette went to dine with friends, leaving us alone. Simon surprised me saying that the staff had the night off too. He produced bracelets, diamante but on a sturdy base, which snapped shut on my wrists with a little click. I was immediately aroused, a sharp pain of passion rising from within. He ordered me to stand still, and he threaded red ribbon through loops attached to the bracelets. Slowly he removed all my clothing. Picking me up, he laid me upon the bed, spreading my arms and legs. 'Don't be afraid, I shall not harm you Trudi.'

I lay impassively, yes frightened with this turn of events, but also so aroused that I did not want to resist. He tied each ribbon to a bedpost, and did the same with each leg. I lay completely nude except for the bracelets and anklets. He thrust a finger into my clitoris and I writhed with instant ecstasy. I was surprised at my reaction. He laughed pleasantly. 'You are very wet you naughty girl. You really like this don't you?'

'Baise moi,' I pleaded.

'Not tonight Trudi, I have other plans for you.' He produced a hand held machine, the size of an electric shaver but with a triangular projection from which a piercing light issued. It buzzed and I was afraid.

He placed himself on the bed then and moved the light across my pubic area.

'What?' I asked tremulously.

'I don't want you to have pubic hair and I am removing it by laser. You will eventually look much more beautiful.' He passed the light several times and I once experienced a slight burning sensation. He stopped. 'I can see it is hurting a little. Would you rather I did not go on?'

'No, I want you to do what you want with me Simon.' How I enjoyed his power over me.

'I'll get you a drink.' He was gone, leaving me time to think. I was so surprised by this new side of Simon, but an animal within was ecstatic at this turn of events. He returned with a cocktail glass of green liquid and I thought back to when I had last been given a green cocktail with Tom. It was not the same. He raised me up with one hand and held the glass for me to drink.

'Take it all,' he said.

It was mint and I thought rum and very strong, with a slightly bitter after taste. It aroused me even more. He bent his head to my crutch and licked away my cum. I was on fire within. This was the best sensation I had ever experienced.

The room swam, the drink must have been very strong. I dreamed, a figure in white appeared as if through a mist and I floated. I have died I thought.

I awoke to find myself alone. The bracelets and anklets were gone. It was still dark and the room was lit by a small table lamp. I was sore in my pubic region. I felt myself. All trace of hair had gone. I thought he had waxed me and that had left me sore. I rose and went to the mirror to see. Where hair had been, already trimmed down to a small triangle by waxing, there was now none left. At first I thought there was, because there was shadowing. I went into the bathroom, into the strong light and found Simon lying in the bath, smiling at me.

'Do you like it?' he asked.

I looked in the full-length mirror. Where the hair had been, I now had tiny entwined red poppies on rich green stems. My pubic area had turned into a little posy.

'That is the latest thing, several of the models have done the same and it is my present to you. You have to take care of it, keep it clean and wipe it with spirit every day until it has healed. I hope you like it.'

'Did you drug me?'

'So that you would have no pain.'

'I wanted the pain. I am ashamed to say, I wanted you to hurt me.'

'It would have been too much. So you like pain?'

'My brother once tied me up and spanked me, for being what he called a cocksucker. I loved it. I still love that sensation of helplessness, of being completely at someone's mercy. I had a friend, her husband tied her up and left her while he went to the pub for an hour or two. I was horrified. Now I understand.'

'So, this is all new Trudi. You have grown up, suddenly no longer the ingénue. Do you like it?'

'I love it. It means I belong to you. Have you done this to Catherine?'

'Oh no. I have to talk to you about Catherine. Annette has told me much, but I also suspected that she was an enemy for you. I am afraid I have made a misjudgement there. Living in the Château has turned her head, but we shall find a way. Do not worry about her, it will be all right.'

'She said I should leave you alone and find a pervert like me to live with.'

'You are not a pervert, do not ever think that. She is more cruel than I thought. It is a bad misjudgement on my part. Well we will see. Of course your artwork is not finished yet. When all trace of hair has gone, then we will finish the work of art. But it is a good start, with the best dyes that hold their brightness. I shall always think of your little posy when I think of you, and you will see it and think of me and this night. Tomorrow, Jean Luc arrives for the last two days?'

'Yes, mon cher.'

'Bon.' He rose from the bath and I towelled him down, loving being there, completely nude except for my posy. His penis was fully erect and I took him again in my mouth until he gasped and came, pumping down my throat and I loved it, loved serving him and came myself. As I fell asleep, his arm around me, with his penis between my thighs, I realised I had never been so happy.

Chapter 8.

Jean Luc appeared before eight, clad in typical French skiwear, functional, old and of an unknown make. He looked young and handsome, and Simon shook his hand vigorously. He then questioned Jean Luc on his home and where his father worked.

We all had breakfast and it was agreed that Jean Luc would ski with Liz and me, taking me today over the mountain and into La Tania. They warned that the slope was steeper, but said they were confident I could manage it.

We skied to the centre, and took a lift to the right hand side. It went ever so high up the mountain and all the time I thought, what goes up must come down, so there would be a long descent. Jean Luc, smiled as I launched myself off the lift, following Liz who skied backwards watching me. Jean Luc skied off, seeming to pick up speed effortlessly, buzzing around us like a horse fly. At first the slope was no worse than I had been down before, then it became really steep and Liz constantly coaxed and urged me on. Jean Luc gave encouragement as he zoomed by. We descended until we turned left into a narrow flattish path, but this fooled me into thinking it was easy. On the side was a steep drop and I was frightened of going over the edge. Jean Luc skied past, and shouted to follow him. I tried to follow in his tracks, imitating his actions as best I could, while Liz urged me on. We came to a steep open slope descending to a lift head and beside a mountain restaurant. I did two turns then fell. Jean Luc stepped up the slope, pulled me up and dusted me down.

'You should not do that,' he said, 'it can be painful.'

'Thank you, Jean Luc. You are really helpful.'

'Look, trust your skis. If your legs tighten up you will fall over and feel tired quickly. You just have to relax.'

He was off down the slope, leaving me to Liz and fate. Soon we were in the trees, a wide piste, steep in parts but I zig-zagged my way down. Jean Luc had disappeared only to reappear above me, having been all the way down and come back. Eventually I reached the bottom, almost exhausted, but I had done it. Liz suggested we have a coffee. Jean Luc zoomed off again, leaving us to our refreshments.

After that the skiing went better. Suddenly I had more confidence, realising that I was not necessarily going to fall, and if I did, the odds were that I would not hurt myself if I just threw myself on my side. We took off and headed for 1650, where Liz said, there were good long easy slopes for me to practice on. We lunched on the slopes. I went to the toilet and rediscovered my posy. I giggled and Liz in the next cubicle asked what was funny.

'Oh, just that I am really enjoying all this. I am crazy.'

'I think so, just a little.'

In the afternoon I resumed and by lift closure was really, as I thought, zooming down the slopes. Jean Luc still skied three times as quickly.

After a vin chaud and amusing tales from Jean Luc, we said goodbye to Liz for the last time. Tomorrow I would ski with Jean Luc and the rest. I showed him to his room and made him comfortable, before going to have tea with Simon, Gérard and Annette. Jean Luc joined us in a couple of minutes. He gave a good account of me.

We went to our rooms to shower and change. Simon insisted on inspecting my posy. He kissed it. 'It looks well,' he said, 'our little secret.'

It all felt quite sore.

After we had showered and as I sat in briefs and brassiere, he gave me a little box. I opened it to find a golden egg, elongated on one end with a little golden chain attached.

'What is it?' I asked.

'Put it in your vagina. I like to think of it safe inside you. It is valuable. Oui, come lie on the bed and I will do it.'

I lay, legs bent and received my gift. Gently he inserted it, pushing with his finger until it was in as far as it would go.

'Is it OK? It does not hurt?'

'No. It is a little uncomfortable, but I can get used to it. What is it for?'

'You will see, soon. Make your face. Be beautiful, wanton, like the makeup you had on the catwalk.

I did as he bid. I had finished and had done my hair and was just picking up my dress when I received a jolt in my abdomen. The egg was not only vibrating but tiny pinpricks of pain, like pins and needles shot across my stomach. I groaned and the pain instantly stopped.

'Do you like that? I would like you to keep it in at dinner, so that I can play with you. The minute I think you are flirting, I will remind you, that I am your king. A bit of fun.'

For some reason I kissed him. What was happening to me? I had been so strong, now I was like his puppet and I liked him pulling on my strings. My knickers were already damp.

Dinner was a struggle. Every time Gérard spoke to me and I was about to answer, the pain commenced. I could hardly eat. I tried not to display any distress. Simon had hidden depths, I was finding out, but the more he inflicted pain, the more I liked it. I took a paper handkerchief from my bag and surreptitiously inserted it in my knickers to soak up my cum. I was sure someone would smell it. It was a difficult meal.

After dinner we played Jengo, which of course I was rubbish at as each time I pulled a brick, I received a jolt in the vagina. Even as I kissed them all good night, my tormentor disciplined me.

In the bedroom, I fell into his arms in exhaustion. His hand was under my skirt, feeling me, his fingers tickling my clitoris, his mouth on mine, his tongue within tying my tongue in knots. We'd had a prolonged love making in front of the company and he was not letting it stop now. I just now needed him to fuck me, and fuck me hard. I begged him to remove the egg and to enter me but he would not. He removed my dress, leaving me in bra and briefs, and clamped the bracelets and anklets on me again. He soon had me tied down on the bed, completely at his mercy and I moaned with pleasure. I begged him to do me, baise moi, I pleaded again and again, but he just sat reading, occasionally activating the egg.

Eventually, he put his papers aside and undressed. He held his erect penis over my face, tantalising me with it, running his hand up and down the inside of my thigh, until I thought I would burst, occasionally activating the egg, watching my face and enjoying my every reaction. At last he allowed me to suck and I took him greedily, discovering that he tasted of mint. I sucked as if a child with a stick of seaside rock and he came into my mouth. I swallowed gratefully.

At last he reached down and pulled on the little gold chain that was attached to the egg and slowly withdrew it, leaving it activated as he did so. The pain grew ever stronger, then it was out and he drew it slowly along the clitoris, setting me afire. He entered, and started to pump, slowly at first and I took up his rhythm, the mattress bouncing with us. 'Oh please,' I gasped, 'please no more, yes go on. Finish me, do it please Simon, Monsieur le Comte, please.'

At last it stopped and I lay gasping covered in sweat, my heart pounding, my body twitching as though I was still receiving tiny shocks. I was exhausted, a rag doll in his hands and there was no escape. He kept on running his hand along my thigh and every now and then, continued into my clit. He kept is mouth on mine, but gently now, so gently that his lips just brushed mine, setting up the tingling tickling he had done before. The sensations were unbearable. He lounged by my side, continuing his tantalising, watching my reactions and smiling as I writhed in tormented ecstasy.

'Please, no more,' I begged. 'it is enough.'

'If you are sure. But I leave the egg, safe inside.' He reached into the bedside drawer and pulled out a box. He clicked open the bracelets and anklets and I was free to open the box. The necklace I revealed glittered even in the dull light of the bedroom. It was a beautiful modern piece that completely circled my neck.

'For being such a good lover and enjoying my games. Diamonds and sapphires. You are OK? I have not harmed you? You enjoyed being my toy, yes?'

'I loved it. With you, it was just so wonderful, but I think you are a relative of the Marquis de Sade.'

'If I had been the Marquis, then I would have hurt you, but I am not, and here we are, you are unhurt and still loving me, I hope.'

'Of course mon amour, le Comte. I am going to the bathroom to shower if you have finished your torture. Then I am going to put on my best nightdress and hopefully, go to sleep.'

Chapter 9.

Thankfully, my lover tormentor allowed me to sleep. I had climbed into bed demurely clothed in my full length cream silk nightdress and made no move to touch him. I was too exhausted and I was also sore, of mouth and nether regions.

He too seemed satiated. I went to sleep quickly, immensely happy but very tired, physically and mentally. In four days time, we would be in class again, and I needed to gather my strength, for the battle to survive this first year would go on. In the morning I explained to Simon how demanding the course was and how hard Jean Luc and I had to work.

We skied together all day, sometimes one waiting for me to catch up, sometimes another. We lunched in Meribel, then trekked back taking the easy route. I was very tired.

Next morning, Jean Luc and I were deposited at Moutier station and took the train to Paris. I was quiet on the journey, and caught my companion looking at me quizzically. He asked if I was ill? I replied that I was just tired. L'amour he said.

We arrived at the apartment sometime after four and I prepared a meal from what we had, the remains of a stew I had made and frozen, some frozen peas and boiled potatoes. It was enough to keep us going. I went to bed at eight after a long soak in the bath. Tomorrow it was back to normal.

Suddenly the university seemed deserted. The intake which had been nearly two thousand was now reduced to around four hundred, all those who had failed the December exam, having been forced to leave. There was less pressure and it was easier to study. Élise had survived and she attached herself to us, so that we now had three chances of hearing the lecture and deciphering notes etc. She had been home to the farm outside Chartres for Christmas, but seemed quite glad to be back in Paris. After lectures we three would sit in a café checking each other's notes and making sure we all agreed. It was the only way in the confusion of French medical school. Next year, Élise informed us would be much easier, because only a hundred or so would survive to go on to second year. Jean Luc and Élise became an item, and sometimes she would stay over with him. I did not mind but I pleaded with him not to desert me. My French was improving all the time, but there were gaps and anyway, we all needed each other.

As a relief from study, I signed up to a ballet class, upstairs in Rue Renaud. It was extremely hard work for a newcomer, but Madame Simonde was accommodating, pleased to have a minor celebrity as a client. She must have been seventy, but was still light on her feet. Gradually, I became more supple and my deportment improved immensely.

I tackled my tenant, asking him to stay.

'Why would I desert you,' he replied, 'I like you and this is the best apartment. We work well too.'

I was reassured.

Slowly the year ground on. Paris came to life again in the spring, and then it was summer. We sat our end of year exams on which our future as students depended. We compared notes afterwards. We all felt that we had done well enough. A week later we found that we had all passed.

Our reward was to serve a month, unpaid as a nurse in hospital. We were all sent to different areas, but we swapped notes when all home together. It was tough. We had all the menial tasks of a ward to do before moving on to less distasteful tasks, but it gave us all a confirmation that this was really the career we wanted.

Jean Luc departed for Bourg-Saint-Maurice and Élise for Chartres. I was alone again. I packed a bag and headed for England. I had not seen my parents for ten months. They welcomed me home with tears of joy, glad to have their Trudi there at last.

My brother appeared, tanned from service in Afghanistan. He seemed much older than his 25 years. He had done things I knew, that none of his family would fully understand, but he only spoke about people, not his work. He looked at me with the same look he had always had, puzzled, unable to understand what he saw.

'I was wrong,' he said, 'you should have been born a girl. I did not understand.'

'You were just a boy. Whenever did a boy understand a girl anyway?'

Vanessa rang inviting me to Normandy to be with her and Claire who had now completed her GCSEs. Ellie was abroad somewhere in the Middle East, now working for the BBC and frequently on television, dressed in battle fatigues as violence and revolution spread like a fever across North Africa. It was strange seeing my lesbian lover there on TV, serious and under fire. It was almost impossible for me to connect the two images. I would miss her, but at least I would not have that complication. I had not seen Simon either, but he had written frequently of the birth in March of twins, a boy and a girl. He was a proud parent, emailing me photos, even though the poisonous Catherine was in some of them. The one thing I did do, was finish what he had started, having all pubic hair removed at a salon. My posy was now perfect and a constant reminder of Simon.

The craziness of Courchevel and the sexual pressure he had subjected me to, seemed a long time away. In Normandy with Vanessa and Claire, who had now grown into a beauty, we led a quiet life. We made two trips to Paris, to do shopping and to use invitations to fashion shows, but I was not asked to model, nor did I want to. No longer did Vanessa want me to service the French fashion houses. I maintained my style, but I was glad to have no pressure. Élise emailed that she and Jean Luc had been to her aunt in the Pyrenees

Vanessa took us to dinner and I found Simon there too. He had flown in from Rome and would fly out tomorrow to New York. He told us of the twins and their mother. He was very proud and relieved to now have two heirs to the estate. Catherine was well, he said. He fondled me under the table, kissed me as we parted, and we went our separate ways.

I lay awake, half expecting him to sneak in, but I remained alone. In the morning we returned to Normandy. Claire had become a serious young woman. She told me she wanted to become a barrister. She was now quite affectionate towards me, wanting to know all about my life in Paris. I made it sound very dull, and on the whole it was. Our time in Normandy without the vivacious and wicked Ellie was rather dull too.

Two days after I returned to Paris, Ellie turned up, just for an overnight stay. Of course she demanded intimacy. She felt me devoid of hair, then looked and was amazed by it. She stripped the sheet from me and shone the light, tracing round it with a finger.

'Why did you do that?' she asked.

'Simon did it to me. I found out he is very demanding, very funny. He likes to have power over me.'

'Really! He was so serious, the perfect gentleman. What else did he do?'

'Oh nothing much. Just what some lovers do. Domination, but never hurtful. Just a complete turn on.'

'So my little Trudi. You like to be dominated?'

'By him, yes. I don't know what happened. One minute it was just straight sweet love, then he was doing just as he wanted with me, keeping me at fever pitch for hours.'

'How?'

'I'm not saying, and I don't think you could do it, because Ellie, much as I love you, you are not the same as him.'

'I love your posy. That is spectacular. Well done Simon!'

Ellie did her best to arouse me, but I reacted half-heartedly. Simon and his tricks had me in his power. Ellie departed for Lincolnshire and Jean Luc came back. He asked whether Élise could share his bed? I said I would discuss it with them.

Next day we met her in the Tuileries. They kissed. Élise kissed me. 'Here's the deal,' I said, 'You pay me a nominal rent, say seventy percent of what you now pay, enough for food and a share of heat etc. You respect the flat, only make love in your room and do not make me feel uncomfortable. Whatever you see, whatever you find out about me, is only shared between us. It stays in the apartment. No gossip, pas bavarder. Jean Luc has been a good friend and I am sure you will be too, but I am vulnerable and gossip could get us thrown out. Simon's wife already hates me, so I have to be careful.'

'Of course Trudi. Les trois Musketeers, all for one and one for all,' Élise said.

'And we work together, for each other, to get through our studies.' I added.

'Yes, three brains are better than one. A syndicate.'

We all shook hands then kissed.

'Now I am buying lunch, to cement our new alliance. Allons-y!'

Élise moved in two days later, much to the disapproval of Madame Gameau. A day after that, we were back to work.

The hospital was full again with the new intake, but as year twos, our lectures were much less of a muddle. We actually had tutorials, ten or fifteen of us at a time with a professor. Elise was impressed with the way my French had developed. She could still hear my accent but my word power was much better and my use of colloquialisms made my speech less stilted. Ellie had amused me, because she said, I even spoke English now with a beguiling Parisian accent. It made me even more femme and irresistible. I liked that. Even though Simon was with the Witch of Beauvonne, I was supremely happy.

Simon arrived the second of October and announced that he was going to stay with me. Catherine was pregnant again and staying at the Château. She had employed a nanny and they were very close. In the day he was very busy and sometimes would slip into my bed late at night. It gave the three of us time to study.

On the Saturday, he demanded that I spend the weekend with him, at the House of Beauvonne. He showed me the new creations.

He pulled a wedding dress from the rail, ivory silk, twenties retro, fitted to about six inches above the knee, then flared out in panels to the floor with a two foot long following train. The back was cut to the waist, but filled with gossamer chiffon. The front plunged between where my breasts would be. I loved it and told him so. 'It would please and amuse me, if you would model it. And this too,' he pulled a black dress in almost the same cut, but the flare was only to four inches below the knee.

'They are gorgeous. But have you not other models who could do this?'

'Of course, but I would like you to do this. One morning is all. Your friends can show their notes of the lecture, and we will take Jean Luc and this Élise to dinner.'

It was too tempting to refuse. My friends agreed to fill the gaps for me.

The rehearsal took place at night and the show opened in l'Olympia, Boulevard des Capucines, not far from the apartment. I loved the whole thing, the clothes, having my hair done in an unusual style, and the makeup. My friends came to the rehearsal and said they hardly recognised me. I looked a different person, far removed from the everyday Trudi they lived with.

The show was very exciting the largest show Beauvonne had put on for three years. All went well, no falls. There were gasps at my dresses and applause when we mass paraded the catwalk at the end. I just loved it. The cameras loved me, and my outfits. It was hard to come down after the show. Madame Dufour was there, the journalist I had met in a bar a year ago, so was Annette. Simon was busy after the show, but Annette came back stage and asked me to go to lunch with her, heading off the ambush from Dufour.

'So how are you Trudi. You looked spectacular. The show was magnificent.'

I told her that I had never been happier. Life just got better and better.

'Now remember back to Christmas at the Château. I mentioned a protégé of Catherine's who had disappeared? Well, she has reappeared. Imagine my surprise when I was at the Château in August. The nanny is Françoise Clement, the girl friend. It will be interesting to see what happens.'

'Does Simon know?'

'I suspect so, but he says nothing. However, I think that as part of the bargain, he is allowed to see you more, that is why this time he has stayed with you. He has stayed out of Paris as much as possible, because you were declared taboo by Schûster.

'I gather that the skiing was a great success for you. You enjoyed yourself.'

I laughed. 'I do not give out secrets, even to you Annette. You know that I enjoyed myself.'

'We could tell, by the yells and screams. Gérard was quite jealous. Simon must be a good teacher, we had thought him rather dull. So what do you do while he is away?

'I live like a nun. I study and eat, and try to ignore the sounds coming from the spare room, Jean Luc and Élise. The high moments make up for the day to day drudgery, but I am very happy.'

'Good I am pleased. Oh God, Dufour has tracked us down. She is coming over.'

'Fancy seeing you here,' Dufour said, pulling a chair. 'Do excuse me Trudi, but I just have to say what a triumph for you. It was marvellous and your two dresses, the pinnacle of what was a most successful show.'

'Madame Dufour is it? I remember we met, oh over a year ago. Fancy remembering me.'

'Fancy you remembering me. I was intrigued that you were modelling again. Are you still a student médicin?'

'Of course, this is my second year.'

'But you found time from your study to do this show.'

'I am not a person of means. I have to earn a living and I could work nights in MacDonalds or every once in a way, do this. Modelling is much more fun and rewarding.'

'Of course. Do you have a boy friend?'

'Alas no Madame. My flatmate and his girlfriend live with me but I have no such attachment.'

'Do you see a lot of de Beauvonne?'

'Unfortunately not Madame. He is away a lot or at the â with his wife and the twins. He is a family man now, you must know, it has been all over the magazines, hasn't it? When he asked me to help with his show, it was the first time in nine months that I have seen him. He looks very well, does he not? Marriage obviously suits him, doesn't it Annette?'

'Oh I believe so. Catherine keeps him busy and he is devoted to his babies.'

'Well look for photos in the newspapers and magazines tomorrow. I am sure there will be plenty of such a beautiful young person as you Trudi.'

'Merci Madame, I thank you for the compliment, but makeup can do wonders as you very well know. Bonjour Madame.'

We watched as Dufour walked away, phone already to her ear.

Annette was watching me. 'Well done. You managed her very well, turning every remark she made. You are quite exceptional. Well Trudi, I must go as well,' she said when we had finished our wine, 'I will see you tonight at dinner. Au revoir.' We kissed and I made my way to the apartment.

In the evening we dressed. Jean Luc had his dress suit and I gave Élise choice of any dress in my wardrobe. Simon surprised me by bringing home the black and red cocktail dress I had worn at the show. He had several orders for copies, already.

I dressed to his command. He watched my every movement, from the shower we shared to pulling on my best black underwear. He insisted on putting on my thong, admiring my posy and running his finger up my clit. I moaned and he laughed. His teasing was cruel, but it made me ecstatic.

'Wait,' he said sternly. 'Where is your egg?'

'In the drawer, must I?'

'I think so. I want you to be wet all evening.'

'I won't be able to eat.'

'You do not need to eat, you need to please and be pleased. I want to put it in.'

I lowered my thong again and he carefully tested and inserted my egg. He pulled the thong up, running his finger around the elastic on the legs. He surveyed the result. My posy could be seen through the lace of the thong.

'I have another wish,' he said. 'Your posy should be in a frame, in the shape of a heart. I have heard of a new process but it does hurt, so they would give you a local anaesthetic. Will you allow it?'

'You know I am yours, as long as it is safe.'

'Oh yes it is quite safe. It will be beautiful. We will do it tomorrow.'

We went to dinner, the four of us and all the models and salon staff, right down to the newest apprentice. It was held in a restaurant close to l'Olympia, which was also just round the corner from Maison Beauvonne.

It was excruciating, trying to maintain my composure as my lover controlled me via the egg. I went to the toilette and removed the egg. I resolved, I would never let him use it again

We left at 23.00, leaving the staff to their fun. At home he undressed me. He was disappointed to find no egg.

'Never again Simon.'

'Have I done wrong.'

'Oui. I like to share experiences with you. This has been fun and I love you, but I am my own person, free to love whoever I want. I love you but I do not want to be dominated by anyone again. I am sorry.'

'Trudi, do not be sorry. I love you. If I had thought that you did not enjoy my little game, I would not have inflicted it on you.'

We talked for ages about my medical training and my family. Suddenly I was missing my mother, something I thought I would not do. I tried to explain how I felt about her, how as I grew up, I had such diverse emotions about my parents. Now at a distance I saw them in a different light, struggling to understand me.

At last we were in bed and I was allowed to sleep. It was ten o'clock when I awoke.

Simon was already up. He brought me breakfast and stroked my breast through the silk nighty. 'Thank you darling, for allowing me to do what I like. You must always tell me if there is something you don't like me to do. You have been wonderful. Now today, we have this little thing to do. So dress in a skirt. They will explain the process and if you do not like it, then you just say no. But it would be amusing.'

We went to a place in a street I did not know. We climbed stairs and arrived on a bright landing that compared to the rest of the building was modern and airy. The receptionist ticked off a name and we went to an anteroom, cream leather and modern pictures. A woman in a nurse's uniform entered and produced a book of photos. She explained that what they did was use a gold dust to make a little frame for the posy. It was she said, 22 carat, almost pure, but a special alloy that would do no harm while remaining bright. I looked at the pictures. It was fascinating. Simon looked at me and raised an eyebrow.

'Leave us please,' he said to the nurse, 'while we discuss this.'

When she had gone, he said, 'What do you think? They will make it around the posy, then you will be complete. It will be discrete, you can still wear a bikini and it will not show. It will not interfere with love making or anything else.'

'Let them do it, Simon. If it pleases you.' I felt a rising excitement within.

Ten minutes later and I was on an operating table covered in a green sheet except for the area they were operating on. I received two tiny pricks each side, with the local anaesthetic. Then they just worked away for about half an hour. The only sensation was a pulling at my flesh. Finally they swabbed my flesh and checked for bleeding but all was apparently well. They held a mirror so I could see. It was incredible. Somehow the posy looked even more impressive. Simon stepped forward in a mask.

'It is good. I love it. Do you?'

The gold was rich and yellow. The posy looked fresh within. It was pretty and it was so intimate

'Yes Simon. I do.'

'Bon. Merci, ' he said to the staff and I was helped up. I was given some fluids to bathe myself and asked to comeback if there was any redness or soreness. After sales service I thought.

We emerged into the sunshine of the street and walked a few yards and I found we were in the Champs Elysée. We took a seat at a café. Simon spoke to the waiter and he brought us champagne and lobster. It was gorgeous. All the time though, I was thinking, no one knows what this young beautiful woman has down there. I glowed within at the thought. What would mother say? Well she would never know. Nor would all those boys at school. I had come a long way and, yes, I was proud of the way I behaved. In my public life, I was a model citizen, a good student, law abiding. In my private sex life, I was like a whore, but only with one man. I did things to please him, allowed things to be done to me that amused him and aroused me. What was wrong with that?

I looked around the room. No one knew that Trudi the model had a posy. I smiled to myself, but Simon was quick to see.

'What is amusing you?'

'My posy and what you have done to me.'

'So does that mean you forgive me?'

'Of course, you wicked man. I love it. Every time I see it, I will think of you. I also think where I have come from. Four years ago, I was a schoolboy. Now look at me. I am overjoyed.'

'I am glad. I love you Trudi. You are all woman to me. Catherine is my wife in name and is bearing another child, but the time will come. My business has never been better, partly due to you, a great box office draw when you model for me. I am very proud of you too, with the way you live and your studies. It is all good.'

'When is the baby due?'

'In February.'

'Do you know what it is?'

'He. A boy, this time we know it is only one, not twins. My family will be complete.'

'And Catherine? Is she happy and well?'

'Oh yes, now she has her nanny. She does not find being a mother easy, but the nanny has taken away the pressure. I know she was not nice to you at Christmas, but I think you will find she has mellowed.'

'She warned me off. She insulted me, called me a pervert and I am not. She said the one good thing about me was that I could not bear a child. I think that is my one tragedy.'

'Yet you said nothing of this to me In Courchevel? Why?'

'Because.........Well, she is your wife and the mother of your precious children. I........, I am just Trudi. I am happier than I deserve to be. My life is magical, so full of highs that I cannot complain. I am not yet twenty. I have strutted the runway, in three different fashion houses. I have clothes more lovely than anyone I know. You have given me jewellery and experiences worth a fortune. I have friends and a brain. I follow my dream to be un médicin and I live in a lovely apartment, rent free in the best area of lovely Paris. I have you, as lover and benefactor. What is there to complain about? Plenty of women cannot conceive, so....'

'I love you for being you, Trudi, but also because you ask for nothing.'

'Only your respect, Simon. That, and your love.'

I was starting to get sore. We bought salt to put in my bath and we went to the apartment. We had dinner, bought in by Simon. I ate in my dressing gown and Jean Luc and Élise shared with us. Simon and I went to bed, not to make love but just to be close.

Sunday morning and Simon departed for the Château. We three took out our books and discussed and consolidated the last week's work.

Chapter 10.

I heard nothing from Simon for a month. Meanwhile we flatmates worked hard as we had to. Although now established as second years, it was still possible to be thrown out. In any case, we all for different reasons, wanted to succeed and to succeed well. I needed success so that I had a career and would be able to support myself in case my dream of becoming a wife, never happened. I had no illusions. Supposedly beautiful I might be, but I knew I was not everyone's ideal partner. Some would never fully accept me, while others would not try to. As a realist, I knew there was a good chance that I would have to remain single. Some would settle for a loveless marriage, but I would rather remain alone than do so.

Jean Luc was really driven. He saw his father working hard and getting nowhere while his mother did menial jobs, cleaning, a bit of cooking, whatever she could find. He had to succeed for his own sake and to help them.

Élise was more of an enigma. Her father was not hard up. He collected her in a four-year old Mercedes and took her home to the thousand-hectare farm. Much as I liked her, she was not contented and I wondered why but did not like to ask.

They were good flatmates. They knew what I had been and it seemed not to matter a jot. They also behaved, cleaned up, washed their bedding and minded their own business I could not ask for more.

It was the end of October when Simon rang. He was coming into Paris and would spend three or four nights with me. I buffed myself up. My hair was now twelve inches down my back and I made an appointment at a well-known salon. I did not have a name to do my hair, that would have really blitzed my bank account, but one of the underlings, I was sure, would do a good job.

I arrived and asked for Marcel who was supposed to do my hair. I was taken to a chair and left waiting for ten minutes. A girl brought me coffee and I read a magazine. I was in no hurry. I like being at the hairdresser, loved, as with the catwalk shows, people titivating me. Perhaps that was why I liked Simon and his tormenting.

I was surprised when I found the owner, Pierre Paquin himself behind me. As with all hairdressers, they do this thing of talking to you through a mirror. I always find it disconcerting. They also discuss one with aids as though one is a package and not a human. Pierre must have sensed my discomfort, because he came beside me and crouched to be at my level.

'Why did you not make an appointment with me, Trudi?'

'I could not afford you.'

'But for you it is different eh. Simon is my friend, we help each other and you are too famous for just anyone to do your hair. So, what am I going to do for you.' He pulled my hair up and let it fall back. 'It is in good condition, some split ends but so has everyone. What do you want me to do?'

'I rather want to keep it long, but I am having dinner with Simon tonight, and I would love to have something special. Can you suggest?'

'First we will wash and trim. The colour is good, it's natural, yes? God has been kind. OK, this is Marcel he will wash your hair, then I will come back to supervise. You will look like a goddess, Trudi. We will do your nails too, and those feet. Ooh, naughty. You are beginning to look like a student.'

I was soon washed. As they straightened my hair, two girls attended to feet and hands. I was in heaven. Marcel and Pierre discussed what they should do for a special occasion. They offered alternatives. I settled for having it up but hanging down the back in ringlets. It was something I had never had before, and of course, I am always ready for new sensations.

After two hours I was done. My toe nails were purple and silver. My fingernails were to match the dress I had selected, a classy silver sheath that I had not worn before, but I knew it was one of Simon's favourite creations. They painted my nails silver, but crackled it to show purple and set diamantes in the half moons. It was very special.

I returned to the apartment to find that my flatmates had gone out. There were still two hours before I expected Simon. I bathed, carefully, so that steam and water would not undo what the salon had done.

I was sitting in the lounge, reading anatomy when my flat mates arrived back from eating at a pasta bar.

'Oh Trudi, big date? Élise asked. 'You look like a princess, doesn't she Jean Luc?'

'Always,' he replied.

At that moment I heard his key in the door, and I shot into the bedroom to do my makeup and dress. It was not long before Simon joined me. He watched my preparations, sitting at my dressing table in the dressing gown. He took that off me as I sat, leaving me sitting in the nude. I did not care. As a boy, displaying my body would have devastated me. As a woman, I could not care who saw me. He swivelled me round to see my posy. I giggled.

He went to my wardrobe and pulled out a bra and a matching string, French, light blue with thin pink ribbons. He selected a packet of stockings and insisted on dressing me. I thought back eleven years to Heather helping me to dress that first time, my tears of humiliation realising that I was somehow wrong, not as others and my fears of discovery of my true self.

Heather now had a child of her own. I thanked Heather in my mind. It had been a good day when I had looked in her pants and that had led to my double life, girl at home, boy at school. All the humiliation, the pointing, the jibes, even the rape by Stuart had been worthwhile, for here I was, a minor celebrity, wealthy due to Simon's support, pampered.

I stood and Simon surveyed me with the same critical eye he used for his models. It was unnerving.

'Do I please you, Simon dear?'

'Of course. You look like royalty. You must wear your diamonds, necklace and earrings and the bracelet. I will change too.'

He disappeared into the bathroom. I heard his razor. He appeared in shirt only, and I giggled. That sight always got me. I sat in the lounge awaiting him. He appeared in a silver grey suit which had a light blue line running through it. His shirt was the reverse, blue but with a grey line and his tie was blue, somewhere between French and navy. His hair was a little more grey at the temples, but still full and just a little unruly. He smelled divine, Gucci pour Homme. He looked like a king. His shirt cuffs showed and I noticed he was wearing the Cross of Lorraine cuff links. I was so proud that I had given him something he valued.

Élise and Jean Luc sat watching us. 'You both look like Royalty,' Élise said.

We took a taxi to Montmartre, a restaurant we had once visited before. Inside we found Pierre and Marco, both of whom I new from past days with Vanessa, and their companions. Everyone kissed. Marco explained that the food here was Breton, fish and beef predominating. Sitting next to me he explained the dishes and advised me. He recommended spider crab to start and I readily agreed. This should be followed by a steak, he said, and chose the Châteaubriand, very rare. Champagne corks popped and the waiter filled our glasses. I found that it was Pierre's birthday, well that was the excuse.

It was a friendly restaurant, small but smelled wonderful. We were a merry crowd. As the youngest and female, I was treated like a pet, the women asking about my dress and where I had my hair and nails done, and the men asking about my studies and telling me that I could make a fortune and never work after being a model.

'Un médicin,' said Pierre, and shivered. 'All that blood and nastiness. You are too beautiful. Why do you want to do that?'

'I want to help people. I was lucky to have someone help me. I want to help others.'

'There are many médicins but as Trudi the model, you are unique, a draw. You would be so in demand.'

'Thank you. I will model for you all if you ask me. I love it. But I must follow my dream too.'

'Bravo Trudi.' Marco's wife said. 'She must follow her dream, but there is no reason why she cannot model in Paris at the same time.'

The crab came, with the other starters. I tasted it and it was just gorgeous, full of flavours of crab and herbs. Some were eating oysters and I was offered one, but I refused explaining that they made me ill.

Then it was time for the main meal. The Châteaubriand was exquisite. People say that French steak is not good, but this was, it had real taste and succulence, melting in the mouth. The men talked business while we talked fashion and shopping. I felt really at ease. These were lovely people. How lucky I am I thought, how much I have to give back for all these bounties that have fallen into my lap. How much I owed to Vanessa for introducing me and to Ellie for taking me to the party where I first met beloved Simon.

His hand often wandered below the damask cloth to fondle my thigh. So he still fancied me. I was relieved and grateful that in this milieu I was fully accepted and valued.

It was after one when we left, but the time had flown by. Paris was sleeping. On Boulevard Haussmann, we saw no one. We went straight to bed.

Chapter 11.

There is nothing as good as waking in the morning beside the person you love, except being beside the person who loves you too. I awoke first and watched him as he slept. It is disturbing if one really thinks about it, but one never really knows what goes on in another's mind. They may say they love you. They may even caress you, but you never know. With Simon I thought I knew that he loved me. His actions told me that he did, but those long silences from him while we were apart. What was that all about? Yet I knew of someone, well Vanessa had told me of him, who had a long affair, yet phoned his wife every night, even in the presence of his lover

I hoped that Simon was true to me. I tested him now. I moved a hand to his groin and felt him come alive. His face also roused lazily from sleep and he spoke my name, my name, not Catherine nor Suzzane or any other female.

I investigated his body further, watching with pleasure as he reacted. His eyelids fluttered and I was on his mouth, parting his lips, inserting my tongue. He reacted slowly.

'So sleepy head, what are we doing today?'

'Today, Vanessa is coming, a surprise for you. We are going to the races at Longchamp. I will select your clothing, a very pretty dress and hat and your highest heels. I want everyone to see you and admire. I have ordered a hamper and we will take the Mercedes limousine. Jerome will drive. Now we have much to do. I have ordered your outfit from the salon, so now we can bathe and get ready. And I have another gift for you today, something I found in India.'

We showered together, washing each other. He selected a brassiere for me, but no knickers. He produced a small box and withdrew what looked like a pile of coins smaller than a five pence piece. It chinked metallically. 'Put these on,' he said, and I was a child again as I leant on him and inserted one leg at a time. Gently and carefully, he raised them up. The waist elastic was tight to take the weight and they felt cold on my skin. He turned me to the mirror. My stomach flipped. It was just amazing what effect this garment had on me. I moved and there was a faint tinkle.

'Yes, it is gold, but only nine carat. You like it?'

'I like everything you give me Simon.'

He went to the front door and came back with three parcels. He selected stockings and watched as I rolled them up my legs. Then he produced the dress. It was retro, just above the knee, a full skirt and full petticoats, with a fitted bodice. It was in grey fine shantung. The shoes matched exactly and with the slight platform were nearly seven inches high.

'Walk for me, remember your training. Oui, that is right. Good girl. Now we try the hat.' He adjusted it on my head, moving it around until he was satisfied then pinned it to my hair. He produced a bag to match. He stood back and surveyed me with his couturier's eye. 'Bon! Look in the mirror. Who is that girl? Why, it's my little Trudi.' He removed the hat. 'Do your makeup. I want classy, not wanton. Look like a young Comtesse.' He watched as I did my face. 'Oui,

OK. Now I dress. Be careful not to spoil. Vanessa should be here soon, you can let her in.'

Vanessa arrived twenty minutes later. She looked adorable in Prussian blue and yellow, a sweet little pillbox with feathers upon her head. She took in my appearance with an appraising eye, demanded that I twizzle round, and then kissed me on both cheeks and my lips.

'My Trudi, you are devine, a real lady. I am so proud of you. I think of you as my third daughter. I just cannot believe that you were that gauche shy boy Stuart brought home six years ago. I am really quite overcome. Is Simon here, ah there you are Simon. Are you satisfied with your protégé?'

'No Madame Vanessa, I am not satisfied. I am ecstatic. This is,' he said, taking my hand, 'the most beautiful girl in Paris, no, in France I think. And she is very good too.' He swept me round so that my skirts rose and layers of petticoat were visible. 'You see how provocative this dress is?'

My knickers tinkled. They were not that comfortable.

'I am impressed by you both,' said Vanessa.

The limousine whisked us effortlessly west and straight into the VIP car park. Simon helped me out and made sure that I looked pristine. He linked arms with us both and we entered the grandstand. Simon seemed to know many people, but then of course, he would, many would be his customers and some his colleagues or competitors. Some called me by name, others he introduced. If it was someone with a title, he demanded I give a small curtsey, and I did my best to please him. I enjoyed being well mannered, dainty and feminine, as well as, yes I have to admit, submissive. He gripped my hand tightly, keeping me close the whole time. I think I kissed more cheeks than an American President kisses babies, but it was just a proximity thing, not actually touching that would disturb my make up. We sat, talking to someone he introduced as the Marquis de Clairvaux. He appeared to me to be very ancient, but his wife looked to be only in her late thirties.

'So, the famous Trudi,' she said, 'you are charming. You are a model still?'

'Yes Madame, occasionally. I am a student médicin at the Sorbonne.'

'Oh, so you have brains too? You are blessed. And you live with Simon?'

'Oh no Madame la Marquise. Le Comte has a wife who is expecting a baby, so she is at the Château. I live in Paris with two students, but Simon is my benefactor and likes to educate me. This is my first visit to the races, and he dresses me for the part. I am very lucky.'

'Madame,' Simon turned to us, 'Trudi is too modest. She is a great beauty, do you not agree? So she shows off my dresses at events like this. I am very proud of her and she is also working hard at her studies.'

'Do you have a boy friend Trudi?'

'No Madame. I do not. I have no time, the study is very difficult especially as French is a foreign language for me.'

She lost interest in me and turned to a woman the other side of her. Simon said adieu and we left to walk further along the balcony. 'That bitch, une putain (a whore), she sold her soul to that old reprobate with his ruined estate. How dare she.'

We found Vanessa with Marco, Pierre and several other fashion personalities. Here we were more at home. Simon gave me a race card and asked me to pick out some horses. I was at a loss, so I looked at the odds, deciding to bet on the second favourite in race one, then the third in race two etc.

Simon placed my bets for me, and we headed to the restaurant, our whole party gathering on one table overlooking the course. I was seated between Simon and Marco again, with Vanessa and Pierre opposite. It was very chic and very merry. Once again I was the youngest and there was a lot of teasing, about boyfriends and of course about being British and being a student médicin. A photographer took pictures of our table, and I asked Simon to buy some for me as a memento. Simon stood and helped me up. He spoke to the photographer and beckoned Vanessa too. We found a spot overlooking the course where we could have photos, and he took a variety of shots of us all or just Simon and I and of just me or Vanessa. I looked at the table and it reminded me of a Renoir, Luncheon of the Boating Party, but more up market.

We resumed our seats. The luncheon was more fun than quality, that is not to say it was bad, just not special. The champagne flowed, but I was careful this time not to drink too quickly.

The first race came and went and my horse trailed in. I then hit a winning streak having two winners and a place in the next three, and a win in the last race. I could not believe it. I looked forward to having a few euros to treat my flatmates to a good lunch.

When the racing had finished, Simon fetched my winnings, thrusting a wodge of notes into my hands. I had €600. Pierre and Marco pretended to make up to me, trying to take my money. Vanessa took me to the ladies. In the cubicle, I lowered the golden knickers, I would be glad to take them off, but they were a thrill too, another little secret thing I shared with Simon. They tinkled as I moved them. We checked our makeup. On the way back, she produced her little camera and snapped me, 'for the family,' she said. 'John will not believe the young lady you have become.' She took me in her arms and kissed me. 'I am so proud that I have been able to help you.'

'Vanessa, you gave me all this. If you had not been so understanding all those years ago, then this would not be happening. You could have been so angry when I borrowed your clothes and Ellie's too, but you saw the real me. That was wonderful of you. John I think, would have put me on a train for home there and then.'

'Ah well, men think differently. He was frightened that Stuart was, well, involved. Simon is good to you?'

'Oh yes. I adore him.'

'Ellie mentioned a posy?'

'Ellie is a very naughty girl then.'

'Even so, I am intrigued. May I see?'

'No Vanessa. It is a private thing, between Simon and me. I worry about Ellie. I hate seeing her in so much danger.'

'It is her choice. I sometimes feel she does not like herself, that is why she seeks danger. She is a grown up. She has always been independent. She loves you, you know. She says you are her ideal.'

'I know. But she is not my ideal. I love her, but I am not in love with her. I do not mind what she does to me, but I will have to speak to her about giving away my secrets.'

Simon joined us from the veranda. 'Come, if you are ready, we go home to change for dinner, all of us at Pierre Gagnaire on Rue Balzac. Trudi, perhaps you like to invite your friends, yes? It would be good to include them.'

'Thank you Simon. I will phone.'

I phoned as we walked to the car, Élise answered. I said that Simon wanted them to come to dinner. She said she had nothing to wear. Raid my wardrobe, I told her. In half an hour we were home and Jerome was released. We would have taxis for the short distance to the restaurant. In the lift, I kissed Simon while Vanessa watched. 'Thank you for a lovely day and for inviting my friends tonight.'

'It is my pleasure. By the way, how are your knickers?' He smiled wickedly.

'Not very comfortable, but I like them.'

'Have you seen them Vanessa.' He raised the back of my skirt with all the petticoats, displaying my gold clad behind.

Vanessa laughed, I giggled. 'He is very naughty, Vanessa.'

'Simon, she will not show me her posy.'

'Ah the posy, C'est magnifique. You can show her Trudi.'

I slipped the golden knickers down for her inspection. 'That really is something. I must have one too.'

'What would John say?' I asked giggling, readjusting myself. We stepped out into the hall and entered my apartment.

Jean Luc was dressing. Élise came with me to my wardrobe.

'Simon, can you pick something for Élise please. And what should I wear?'

Simon picked out an aqua off the shoulder dress for her. For me, he selected my long black gown strapless with a plunging back. He went to his apartment and came back just as I emerged from the shower.

'Do your face first. I will help you with the dress. He selected my underwear, and placed them on the bed. He came back into the bathroom and proceeded to undress. 'Let me look at that posy again,' he said. And I revolved on the seat towards him. He looked and laughed, 'It is pure genius Trudi.'

'So is this,' I said, and took him in my mouth. He gasped. 'No not now, Vanessa is here....'

'So. You want me to, don't you.' I resumed and he came very quickly. He went into the shower and by the time he emerged, my makeup and hair were done. I went into the bedroom to find Vanessa already changed. I put on the knickers and stockings Simon had selected and waited, semi nude for him to help with the dress. He came through in evening dress. He produced tape and scissors. He taped under my breasts so I had uplift, and applied double sided tape to my front ribs for the dress to stick to. It all looked very precarious. I stepped in and he pulled it up, the back only just covered the crack of my bottom. He used more double sided across my buttocks, then drew the dress up zipping the short back zip and fixing it against the tape. He brought up the heavily boned front and fixed it. He tested it experimentally. He placed a string of pearls about my neck and a silver cuff around my right wrist.

'Perfect.' he said. 'Go and look.'

In the mirror I saw Holly Golightly. I smiled and she smiled back. I selected a black chiffon stole and picked up a bag, filling it with things a girl needs, lipstick, handkerchief, a compact, mainly for the mirror, and a tiny hair brush.

In the salon, Vanessa was getting to know Jean Luc and Élise. Jean Luc was very handsome when dressed up. Élise looked lovely. Vanessa was just so elegant in a dark gold gown. Simon was smart and handsome and so desirable. I wanted him to do things to me.

The restaurant was only three minutes in the taxi. The walls were polished wood in the front of house but we were shown to a large room behind, painted in muted colours. We were twelve, the five of us, Marco and Pierre and their wives, a friend of Vanessa, Claude and Pierre the hairdresser and his partner. Simon showed me the menu and I chose, duck on a bed of salad to start and then sole.

Élise was very animated, talking to Pierre and his partner. She was laughing, something she rarely did. Jean Luc was talking to and joking with Marco's wife. The food was gorgeous, and the atmosphere was wonderful. I would remember it all my life.

Simon was his usual attentive self, pulling my leg and touching my thigh. I could see him out of the corner of my eye, watching me. I was disconcerted, but realising I had caught his stare, he pulled me to him and kissed me.

Pierre the hairdresser said, 'ooh la la. C'est l'amour.' Others said, 'Oui, oui, bravo Simon et Trudi.'

I blushed, not knowing what to do.

'Of course I love her,' Simon said, 'I am so proud of my protégée. She continues to please and amaze me.' He raised a glass, 'A toast to Vanessa who introduced us, and to Trudi too, not only a beauty but also clever.'

It was too embarrassing. I turned and put my head on Simon's chest and cried. He wiped my tears with a napkin, then Marco made a joke and the moment had passed.

We returned to the apartment after midnight. Vanessa was to sleep in my bed and I would go to Simon's with him.

His bedroom was furnished in Second Empire style, lots of gold furniture and some chinoiserie. The bed was enormous. The bathroom was very old, looking as though it had been plumbed in the 1930s. The pipes were polished brass, the bath huge too, standing on lion feet.

Simon carefully removed my clothing, and before I could remove my makeup, he picked me up and placed me in the bed. He disappeared and returned nude. He climbed in beside me.

'I am worried,' I said, 'tonight you were more like my lover, than my protector. It was OK, because we were among friends, but if someone tells the media. We had that before, and it was awful, in fact it parted us.'

'Yes, it was not so good, but I am just fascinated by you, the way you deal with everything.'

'So, we must be careful Simon. And there is Catherine too. What would she say?'

'Catherine has her own worries. The new baby is due in just over three months. Meanwhile, she has Françoise to entertain her. I have not slept in her bed for five months.'

'Oh Simon, I am sorry.'

'Well we will see what happens.'

'No Simon, we will not just wait and see. Catherine will have a plan, I know her, so you too must have a plan.'

'We have a prenuptial agreement. If we part, she receives €5 million. That is a lot of money, but I can just afford it. She does not get the Château, nor this house. It is agreed that I will buy her a house in Biarritz. I will contest for the children, preferably having sole access. She is not a good mother and this Françoise and she are lovers. The doctor for the Château and I are keeping records of anything that happens to the children and the behaviour of those two. I let her know that I know what is going on, so that she feels free to do as she likes. However, we always deny that we sleep together, yes?'

'Of course. In future then, we must be truly careful. My friends are fine, but if they were forced to make a declaration, I do not know what they would say. Annette too. Simon, I am very worried. But Simon, I do not believe the children should be deprived of their mother. It is not fair to them or to Catherine.'

'She displays no aptitude for motherhood. Françoise does everything. Catherine does not go near sometimes for days. If she changes, then I change. Do not worry. It will be OK. I have my spies and they have plenty of evidence.' I let it rest, and eventually we slept, without making love. By seven next morning, he had gone. I did not know when I would see him again.

Chapter 12.

Vanessa stayed another two days, sharing my bed. I was at university all day and at night we had work to do. Vanessa looked after herself, seeing old connections and collecting parcels, then she left for Normandy.

It was good to have my privacy again, because our work was still hard. We were told that in the third year, the work eased up, but we had to survive this year. Already by December, eight students had given up. If one fell behind then it was absolutely hopeless to catch up. The Three Musketeers supported each other, they doing more for me, but I at least gave them cheap and up market lodgings allowing them to concentrate on the course. It was therefore a good bargain.

Professor Rousse summoned me to his office. He threw a daily paper across the desk at me, stabbing a photo with his finger. I looked and saw that it was our party at the races. Underneath were our names.

'You prefer the races to study Madamoiselle?'

'No Professor.'

'Then why were you not here.'

'My benefactor demanded that I attend, sir. I do not see him often, so I have to try to please. He has been very good to me, and my friends helped me catch up.

'So, Trudi, le modèle. Give me all the parts of the heart?'

I named them. He seemed unimpressed. 'Give me the important parts of the circulatory system.' I named them as much as I could, hoping I left out nothing.

He put his elbows on the desk his finger tips touching each other forming an A shape.

'You may go now. Be careful. I am watching you.'

'Merci Professor. I am working hard.'

A day later, I received an envelope of photos from the photographer. They were good. As I looked at them, I resolved to have a permanent memento of the day.

On the Saturday morning, the three of us trooped across the Seine to find one of the left bank artists. Eventually we came to a stall of impressionistic paintings. The young man there was the artist. I showed him a photo of the races party and asked him to paint it in the style of Renoir's The Boat Party Lunch. He wanted €200. I gave him fifty down, for materials and promised two hundred more when it was completed to my satisfaction. I gave him my phone number and my name.

I thought no more about it until a phone call a week before Christmas. It was finished he said. We arranged to meet in a cafe close to the Pont Royal. Élise had gone home, so Jean Luc came with me before catching his train to Bourg.

We met Eric Baptiste as arranged. I expected a daub and when he opened his portfolio, I was expecting the worst. He brought out an unsupported canvas and laid it down on the table. I stood to look. I asked him to stand with it while I stood back eight feet, then twelve, the furthest I could stand away. As I retreated, so the scene came to life. There I was, and Simon. Marco was waving animatedly, Vanessa gesticulating, Pierre waving a glass. It was excellent. I willingly paid Eric another two hundred and a fifty pour boire, if he would have it framed in a modern frame and deliver it. He promised to do so, using the art college facilities. I took Jean Luc to the station, treating him to lunch on the way.

We embraced at the station and I thanked him for all his help. I would see him in Courchevel after Christmas, but I gave him the present from Simon and I. It was an envelope, not to be opened until Christmas, but it contained a voucher for ski clothes. We kissed and he dragged his case down the platform.

I returned to an empty apartment and got down to work, revising, making sure I knew everything I should from the course notes. I took two days off trying to find a present for Simon. Marco suggested a dress shirt, and gave me one, the lovely man.

Two days of study, and Simon appeared to take me to the Château. I just loved that ride alone with him. As I climbed from his car at the Château, I realised how damp I was. I still fancied him then. It really must be love. The day was as grey as the walls of the Château. In the sun of summer, the walls looked warm and friendly, but in dull winter light, they seemed to radiate coldness. I was soon installed in the same room as last year. The party was to be the same as last Christmas too, except for Françoise Clement. I wondered what I would make of her. At least I would have Annette and Gérard.

I bathed and readied myself for dinner. I held back, hearing the buzz from down in the vestibule, but not wanting to be part of it too soon. I answered a knock at the door and found Annette and Gérard waiting to escort me down. I emerged in a full-length strapless creation in emerald, my hair falling down my back like gold. Head up, I negotiated the stairs, safely, heads turning as the three of us descended the wide staircase.

I went straight to Catherine, kissing her on both cheeks and said I hoped she was well and having a good pregnancy. She forced a smile and said she was well. It was good to see me again, she said.

'How are your studies?'

'Bon Catherine, merci. We work hard.'

'Let me introduce you to a great friend and my nanny.'

A blonde woman, of about thirty-five stepped forward, her hair cut in a short bob. She offered a hand like a wet fish. She had a nice smile.

Gérard collected me, or rescued me and took me to the other side of the room to introduce me to his friend a vigneron with a vineyard in the Bordeaux area. He mentioned some grape varieties, but they meant little to me. At last we went in to dinner, on the arm of Gérard again, and sitting next to Simon. Catherine and Françoise occupied the far end.

Remembering my disgrace of last year, I pecked at each of the seven courses and sipped the wines sparingly. It was marvellous food, but just too much. I would rather have longed for the next course than dreaded it. At last it was over. I pleaded tiredness from my studies and took to my bed early. I wished I was not there. I phoned home. My brother was home for Christmas with his fiancée, Alison. She was, mother said cattily, rather like me to look at, but not nearly so good looking. She was, she conceded a nice girl, but she didn't approve of women in the army, even as doctors.

She missed me, she said and a cloak of guilty selfishness enveloped me. I told her of my studies, but she seemed really to have no conception that I was working hard. I asked after father? Father was well too, she said.

When I spoke to father, he was much more understanding and straight forward. 'It is your life, you have to do what you want with it, but we hope to see you soon.' I promised.

Christmas day. I missed breakfast. Simon sought me out. 'I want you to ride,' he said. He pulled jodhpurs and a jacket from the wardrobe. He had bought me boots, so it was all part of his long-term plan.

At the stable, Sabine had saddled two horses, Simon's large bay gelding and what she told me was my Arab mare. She helped me up. She looked critically at my stirrups and shortened them. 'Toes in the stirrup, heels down. And for goodness sake, straighten your back. Aren't you a model?' Sabine said.

Did she really hate me, I thought?

It felt good being so high up, and I tried to look the part, rather than a sack of potatoes. I smiled at Sabine in spite of her attitude. She took the leading rein and we set off across the park. We rode the other side of the wood.

She set about my education. Walking was not too bad, trotting was horrendous, but she assured me, excellent for the conformation of the legs. We mostly walked and I began to feel and understand the rhythm of the horse. We trotted a little, then she asked if I would like to have a little canter? I said I would give it a go, we set off into a trot and on into a canter, grip with your knees and stay in the saddle, work with the horses motion, hold the reins lower, grab a piece of the main in your hands to keep them steady on the horse, look up, straight back. It seemed that I could do none of these things. It was exhausting but also exhilarating. I wished I had started riding ten years ago. She kept up a constant critique of me and also advice. It was hard to take t all in.

After an hour my hands were sore, my arms felt as though they were coming out of their sockets and my legs felt as if they would be permanently bandy. I was glad to hear that we were returning to the Château, but I was determined to conquer this sport if I could. There were things about it that I loved, the feel of a living creature beneath me, the style and the clothes, and the social aspect. If I were to live with Simon, then I wanted to share everything with him.

Back at the stables, I managed to get myself off the horse.

Sabine smiled. 'Tired?'

'Yes Sabine, I have to say, I think I ache all over.'

'You need to do more exercise, Trudi le modèle.'

'I think you are probably right Sabine. By the way, I am a student not a model. So just call me Trudi please?'

She made no reply except to say, 'OK Trudi. You run along, I will stable these two. I'll see you tonight.'

I gladly left her. Surely she could not be jealous of me. What other reason could there be for her attitude?

I was soaking up so much knowledge I thought sometimes my brain would burst. There were my studies; the French language; just being a young woman, though that seemed easy, etiquette and worldliness, the knowledge of food and wine; how to address different levels of society; what to wear and when and how; and how to accessorise and when not to. I had accomplished much but there was much more to learn. Simon knew so much.

We gathered in the salon early, so that we could open our presents before dinner. Only Gerard and Annette, Catherine and Françoise, Simon and I remained. I had expected Sabine to be there. Simon distributed the presents.

As usual the first two went to Catherine, some great lingerie and a Patek-Philippe watch. He gave Françoise lingerie too.

He brought me a parcel. Inside, I found an Alexander McQueen tote, in tan leather with a silver clasp. I looked inside to see the different pockets and found two boxes, one was an iPad, to help with my studies he said. The other was smaller, a gold Rolex ladies chronograph. I gasped, rose from my place on the floor and kissed him, four times, two on each cheek. I wore the watch then and there.

I gave him the shirt and apologised that it was such a small present.

We went in to dinner. This time Catherine and I were face to face and it was uncomfortable. We both knew each other, and neither of us liked what we saw, but had to pretend. Gérard was the life and soul, and Annette pumped me about my studies and my companions. I spoke too of my brother and his fiancée and their service in Afghanistan. Tomorrow and Courchevel would not come soon enough. It is almost a year, I thought, since I received my posy. A giggle escaped. Catherine was quick to pounce.

'What amuses you?' She did not bother to use my name.

'I was thinking of my brother as an officer and a gentleman, contemplating marriage. He used to be such a dirty urchin.' I lied glibly.

She immediately lost interest. I busied myself with the goose which was delish. After coffee, I excused myself, saying I was tired. I kissed everyone, even Catherine, and took my parcels to my room. Tomorrow we departed for Courchevel, a day earlier than last year, and it would not be soon enough.

Chapter 13.

We left the Château just after six, travelling in darkness for the first hour. Simon continued my education by playing Beethoven, the seventh symphony he informed me. He was in a merry mood and hummed along to some of the melodies, laughing as he found me watching him. He explained that Beethoven was deaf by the time he wrote it, and he depended on the rhythmic nature of it to tell him at what stage the orchestra was playing. I had learned a little music at school, but my knowledge was only fundamental. In the apartment we mostly played pop and rock, and Élise and I would dance around to it. The opening of this symphony reminded me of a dawn awakening and the land coming to life. At first I saw our surrounding countryside but as it became ever more vibrant, I saw my home in Paris and the traffic, sometimes stopped for traffic lights then setting off again in a mad dash to who knows where.

What was best of all was just watching my lovely companion, the cold exterior of home life cast off and his inner joy released. He felt under my mini skirt, and pulled it up to see my knickers. I made no falsely modest attempt to stop him, why should I? I loved his attention.

'Take off your pants,' he said, 'I want to peep at your posy.' And he laughed.

'I want you to keep your eyes on the road, or we shall both be in hospital.' But I did as he asked, flinging the skimpy silk at him. He took them to his lips.

'Fragrant,' he said, then as we were on a straight road, arranged them on his head as a sort of French revolutionary cap. 'Vive l'Empereur.', singing the Marseillaise above the quiet section of Beethoven's symphony.

'Idiot,' I said. I had never seen him so gay. When we first met, he had been sad at the loss of his sibling and his parents. Then he seemed to recover as we grew to know each other, but he was still serious. Now he seemed full of life, though at the Château, he had appeared quite withdrawn.

I showed him the Rolex upon my wrist. 'Thank you.' I leaned across and kissed his cheek. I brought up my tote in its polished leather. 'Thank you.' And I kissed him again. From it I produced the iPad. 'Thank you so much for all my presents, mon amour, Simon.'

We drove listening to the music and I watched as the light came up and colours infiltrated the countryside. Could life be better than this?

Gérard and Annette raced by and we kept pace together as the roads opened up. The duel carriageways were empty as we cruised south and east to skirt Clermont Ferand. We climbed higher and higher, gradually, then after the Clermont turning headed west through the deserted Auvergne. The day had turned sunny, with a few baby clouds bouncing along. We stopped in Thiers centre, just off the E70. He forbade me to replace my pants, but I disobeyed. He was not in a mini skirt.

We ate at the same restaurant as last year, puy lentil soup, and la potée auvergnate, a delicious local stew of meat and vegetables, washed down by a bottle of Saint-Pourçain. We all freshened up. Annette watched while I retouched my makeup. 'Unbelievable,' she said.

'What?'

'You, mon petit chou. You are so, so girly.'

'I am so happy and when I am happy, I am very girly and when I am girly I am happy.'

'And today? What makes you happy today?'

'Everything. My watch and my bag,' I held them up, 'the journey, I love the drive with Simon, and you and Gérard, and cher, cher Simon, who I love, but also, just being me. I am in a good place in my life.'

'And being away from that salope, that bitch?'

'Ah oui. She does not like me, but then if I were her, then nor would I.'

'No, do not feel guilty. She always knew, this was to be a marriage of convenience. Then she got a taste for being la grande dame in the Château, and reneged on the bargain. She knew of Simon's love for you all the time. And she has that petite putain Françoise to keep her company. It is all about the Château and status. You are too good.'

'That girl, Sabine! She seems to hate me too.'

'Oh I don't think so. Her family are related. Her father is Simon's cousin and through some thing in the past, Simon's father inherited the estate. I don't know the details, but there is a sort of feud. Sabine also, I wonder if she is gay. Perhaps she fancies you? She is a clever girl, a first class degree in agriculture and another in economics. She wants to run her father's farm and they have rowed about methods and direction. So she is reduced to being Simon's groom.'

'Oh, she is frustrated. I am sorry.'

We found the men talking in the cool sunlight of the courtyard. We entered our respective cars. Simon asked me to drive for a while. I demurred at first. I had not driven much since arriving in Paris, and this was after all, a Mercedes and large. He insisted so I climbed behind the wheel. We set off at a steady pace through a deserted Thiers and rejoined the motorway. I gradually got the feeling of the big car and we bowled along on the speed limit, being careful not to attract attention after our one glass of wine, for the police had recently become very tough. After two hours as we approached Moutier, Simon said he would drive again. I was glad, because I dreaded the mountain road. It frightened me even as a passenger.

I slept a little, and when I awoke, we were just pulling into the underground garage. Robert was there to meet us and to see to the luggage. Once more we all took the bubble to Jardin Alpin and the lovely Chalet Montagne. It was just light. In the lounge was a roaring log fire, and a cake upon the table and tea and coffee. We ate and chatted about the journey. I was surprised when Annette sitting next to me held my hand. I pretended not to notice, then as she squeezed I looked at her with a quizzical smile.

She addressed Simon rather than me. 'Ce petit chou,' she said, 'is adorable, Simon. You are a lucky man.'

'Oh I know that. You know that at first, it was a matter of sympathy and guilt that I wanted to help her, but that has all passed away a long time ago. Now I am captivated, intrigued, surprised and yes, honoured.'

I blushed. 'No Simon, you honour me. You have literally made me the luckiest girl.' I released myself from Annette's hand and flung myself on his chest, sobbing.

'There, you see Annette, she is human after all. Come, we go up to bathe.'

In the bedroom, we unpacked and I was just about to enter the bath, when I was seized, one hand between my thighs, cupping my posy and the other around my back and his hand cupping my left breast. The room revolved and I landed on my back across the bed. Then he was upon me. His love was savage. It seemed we were performing summersaults as he commanded I adopt different positions. I had not known him like this before, so commanding, so demanding. He wanted me in every way we had tried before. Gradually he became more tender, until he ended by stroking my posy, kissing me and entering me with his tongue.

The power of him had made me completely without a will of my own. I just enjoyed being his reactive plaything. Usually strong and independent, I surrendered myself to his will. Then we were kissing, his lips roved, tickled, pressed. His stubble scraped my skin and the roughness was an added pleasure.

Finally, he ran the bath, lifting me carefully in and washing me, his hand paying special attention to my not so private parts. As I dried myself he quickly bathed, then insisted on dressing me, rolling stockings up my legs, fastening a suspender belt about my waist and attaching the stockings. I was not allowed to do anything. Next came my brassiere, he arranged my breasts within, carefully, making sure my nipples were aligned and rampant. He produced a string of almost transparent silk and black lace to match the brassiere. I was allowed to step into my black cocktail dress with the bouffant skirt with white petticoats, and he zipped it up. It was lovely, but so difficult to sit down in. At least the petticoats hid any sight of my upper thighs or pants. But I loved that dress, real catwalk, head-turning quality.

I was allowed to do my hair and apply my makeup as he dressed. Finally, he produced what I took to be a diamante choker and cuff and a watch, and adorned me as I sat mute, his doll to do with as he pleased. He fastened the cuff on my right wrist, removed my new gold Rolex from my left, replacing it by a silver coloured stone encrusted Omega. He stood behind me with the choker, but before he fastened it he kissed my neck and buried his teeth in my nape. I felt feint. The room swam. He must have sensed my weakness, for his left arm turned and held my waist in one swift movement.

'Oh my darling girl,' he said, 'how would I live without you. You are everything to me. When we met, nearly five years ago, I never dreamt this could happen.'

'Nor I,' I whispered.

We descended for dinner and found Gérard and Annette watching television. Gérard had prepared cocktails, French 75, gin, lemon juice, syrup and topped off with champagne. It was warming and delicious. I sipped delicately.

Annette watched me, seeming amused. 'So Trudi dear, it is nice to be here again isn't it? We are like a family, we four. I love your diamond choker and cuff and that watch. Simon certainly knows how to dress you for the greatest effect.'

'Diamante Annette.'

'No,' Simon said, 'would I give you diamante? They are not the best, but they are not bad. I was going to give you a Mercedes sport, but then you do not drive in Paris, so this is better. And if anything should happen to me, then you would have money in your bank.'

'Let me educate you Trudi. That diamante watch by Omega is platinum, and the face is real mother of pearl and those little stones are all diamonds.. It is worth twice as much as your new gold Rolex. And the silver metal of your cuff and choker are also platinum. As you stand there you are worth an absolute fortune. I must say, I am envious. Simon loves you very much.'

'I know he does, I just didn't expect him to spend this sort of money on me. I cannot respond in kind. Last year I gave him second hand cuff links, this year a dress shirt. I cannot compete and I feel spoiled and greedy, but I truly did not know.'

I had given him a shirt, and that, Marco had given to me.

'It is too much,' I said. 'I have nothing more to give you.'

'You give yourself, it is enough. I like spoiling you.' Without you as a refuge at this time, I would have nothing. You are to me, lover, confidante, little sister and precious. So a few baubles, is little enough.'

I took his hand and kissed it, followed it up with a kiss on the lips. 'I adore you too mon amour.' I said.

The chalet was warm, safe and private. The lights as so often in France, were quite dim, but were nicely placed, so that light bounced off the panelling. The dining table as usual, was set perfectly and we four sat on the long sides opposite each other. Robert had prepared crayfish tails with couscous salad and a balsamic dressing. He followed this with my favourite, magret de canard. It was so delicious, the sauce with the duck had the sweetness of cherries and the succulent juices of the pink duck were just beautiful. We followed it with chocolate fondant. Delicious.

Simon outlined the skiing. Tomorrow the three would ski all day together and I would ski with Liz again. The day after, I would ski with Liz in the morning and we would join them for lunch. Hopefully we would all ski together when Jean Luc joined us. He had persuaded Élise to come to, if Simon agreed. 'Of course,' he said, 'I like your young friends and it is good for you.'

Next day, Liz was a hard taskmaster, telling me that I had forgotten all I had learned last year, making me work really hard. The day was bright and cold, the strong sunlight shimmering off the carpet of sparkling snow. For an hour, she had me on a steep slope, side stepping up and then doing two turns, right and left down it, between the sticks she had placed. It was exhausting. As a reward we drank hot chocolate on the Saulire. We caught the huge and frightening cable car to the top, between fifty and a hundred people crammed in and suspended on a cable. I hated it. We skied to 1650 and its gentle slopes which were excellent, Liz said, for learning and practising technique. I started to abandon fear after two falls, finding that I was not hurt.

'Trust the skis,' said Liz, 'transfer your weight. Look I'll show you what happens. She skied on one ski and it naturally turned, then the other and she turned the opposite way. She made me practice all the way to the village, as many turns as possible. I could not get the one legged turn, but at least I was only using the spare leg as a small prop and putting eighty per cent of my weight on my down side leg. We lunched early before the rush, and were back out onto deserted slopes.

'Quicker, quicker,' she scolded 'yes better, that is right. So now we go to the top of the mountain. It is steep, but just go slowly. If you go too fast, you make a little half stop and point the skis up the mountain to slow, then you do your turn. You will follow me closely. Control your speed all the time. You run into me and I will leave you on the mountain, I mean it.'

We took the giant lift to the top of Saulire again. I tried to appear unconcerned and looked down to see just what I had to face going down. I wished I hadn't. At the top, we walked out upon that steel grating which made me feel sick and I wanted someone to hold my hand. I just wanted to get off. In the press of people, I nearly lost Liz too and started to panic, but there she was waiting patiently. I smiled wanly.

' This is the steepest we have done, but you can do it. Pay attention to the slope. Do as I have told you. Copy what I do, turn in my tracks and control your speed, as I have taught you, you understand?'

'Do a longer turn further back up the hill to slow?'

'Good. We go down here, slowly and then to the left. No matter what happens you follow me. Don't stand looking at it getting frightened, it looks worse than it is and it is wide after this first bit, plenty of room. Follow me or you will get lost. Ready? Off we go!'

I followed down to where several skiers stood looking at the slope ahead, but Liz gave me no time to do that, simply going over the top and putting in a turn. I followed, my heart thumping and a tear in my eye, whether from the cold air or from fear I knew not. I turned where she had and she was already turning again. After three turns the slope decreased and the piste widened. I relaxed a bit more but my legs screamed and burnt and I was out of breath. Just as

I was ready to sit down and cry, she stopped and motioned me to stop beside her.

'Not bad. It's OK. See you can do it. We rest a little. That is the worst bit over. Another fifty turns and we will be at your chalet. Look, you can just see it in the trees, oui, the big one there.' She pointed with her stick. How I longed to be there already.

'OK, we go, or we will freeze. It's getting very cold and it will snow tonight. When I set off, you do to, following still.'

I followed. I thought she would never stop, and my legs burned. Two more rests and we were in Courchevel.

'Good girl. I am proud of you. Now I can collect my bonus from your husband.'

'Not my husband. My benefactor.'

'I was being polite,' Liz said, 'of course, I know who you are. Anyway, well done, very well done. They are meeting us in the Courvoisier bar.' She led me to a smart bar. We locked the skis to a rack outside and pushed our way to the back where we found them. Simon ordered our drinks, and Liz gave him a report on my progress.

'Well it is not yet pretty skiing, but it is coming. We just came down from Saulire, so I am claiming my bonus, Simon. She did well. Now it is practice and I think, skiing with the party tomorrow will do her good.'

'Well done, both of you.' We kissed. We had another drink, and took the bubble to the chalet. Liz would join us for dinner.

After a cup of tea, I went up to our room. I took off my clothes and lay in my underwear. When I awoke, it was quite dark. Simon sat reading on his side of the bed.

'So, awake now. You must have been tired.'

'I was. It was exhausting but exhilarating. I worked really hard.'

'The less you worry about it, the easier it becomes.'

He put down his book. 'Time to undress.' He undid my brassiere and carefully removed my string. He stood looking down at me.

'Very amusing, your posy. I think of it all the time. Have you brought your egg?'

'No Simon. I knew you would want to tantalise me. Such a bully you are. I do not like it.'

He shrugged, 'OK. We will not dress, just casual for Liz will not dress so it would be unfair. Just put on one of your little mini skirts and hold ups and that nice chiffon blouse you have. Where did you get that?'

'NafNaf. I like that shop.'

'So let us shower together. We have some fun tonight after dinner, now you are rested, or you will not be able to sleep.'

We showered and dressed. He stroked my posy. He shook his head, and turned away, laughing gently. 'Perfect.'

'You are proud of that, aren't you.'

'I love it. I like thinking about it, and I love you too for allowing it.'

'If I remember right, I was asleep at the time. Drugged!'

'So, you don't like it?'

'I love it too. It reminds me of you and how good but wicked you are. I thought I should do the same to you, perhaps an elephant's head with your penis the trunk.'

'Very amusing, but you would have to catch me first young woman.' He chuckled and shook his head.

'Simon, I have not said, but I am sorry you are so unhappy at the Château.'

'It will be resolved. Once my new son is born, then we can make new arrangements. I have employed Annette as my PR guru. I also have a new designer at the salon, working on a new range alongside Jacques who will design his ranges, but I am going after the street fashion market, see what is happening in London and translating it into designs for shops like your NafNaf. Haute Couture is not of so much interest for them these days. Fashion is happening on the street.'

'I love my haute couture, and modelling. It is so special. But all that business does not solve the problem of Catherine and the arrangement that you have made with her, for another six years too.' çç

'I feel that things will be resolved before that. I just ask you to be patient. You have been, you ask for nothing, just trust me for bit longer.'

'It is not that I don't trust *you*, nor ask for *myself*. You have given me a very good life, I am so lucky. But you are unhappy, that is my worry. Living with the oppression of Catherine and that Françoise too! It must be torture.'

Simon bent and kissed my hair. 'You are special. You worry about me, but you must not. Catherine can be bought off. I regard this situation as bargaining. She has developed a taste for being the Comtesse and a kept woman. She is unlike you, avaricious, vindictive and ruthless. She just soaks up everything as if by right. You enjoy everything I give you but ask for little. It is my pleasure to spoil you, but you have not become proud. She is proud, haughty and rude. It will be resolved. It is a matter of money. Enough of that salope!' Tomorrow your friends arrive. I hope Élise can ski?'

'Jean Luc tells me so. I don't know how well, but I believe she has skied several times.'

'Good, I will arrange lunch for us all.'

I said no more but I worried about the situation at the Château. We found Liz had arrived when we entered the lounge.

'Tomorrow,' she said, 'you have to pay attention to style. No more going down hill like a hairpin. You are a model after all. Simon, I think we will put books on her helmet for her to balance.'

They all laughed.

'You laugh now. I will show you.'

'I think Trudi is tired. You go up ma chère. I will not be long.' Simon said.

Chapter 14.

He was not long in appearing. I pretended to be asleep, my nightdress plainly in view. He went to the bathroom. Through closed lashes, I watched as he emerged from the bathroom and quietly climbed into bed.

When he had put the light out and settled, I erupted. I grasped him firmly and felt him come alive in my hand. I moved across and bit him on his nipple, making him gasp. I settled on top, guiding him into me.

'You devil, did you think you could sleep without paying proper attention towards a young girl.'

'I am sorry Trudi. I was a naughty boy. What should I do?'

'Baise-moi!'

Slowly, I bounced upon him, stopping to kiss his dear mouth, his hands upon my breasts, cupping them, pulling at my nipples, his hand around my bottom and thighs. When I sensed he was about to come, I would stop, tantalising him, so that he begged me to go on. I managed to stop three times, before I too, wanted that sweet pain and we came together. I collapsed upon his chest and was asleep before I knew.

Wakening later, I found us still joined. I smiled and fell asleep again till the cold light of a snowscape crept around the fold of the thick drapes. I found him watching me as I awoke, and he reached for me and pulled me close. I put my right leg across his and we lay tightly together, just hugging, feeling the life of each other pulsing.

Élise and Jean Luc arrived for breakfast, Jean Luc sporting a new ski suit, for which he thanked Simon. Simon presented Élise with a handbag as a late Christmas present so that she was not left out. She showed me her hand, and she was wearing an engagement ring. I kissed them both and showed Simon.

'Tonight we celebrate,' he said, 'Congratulations.' Everybody embraced.

Breakfast was extra special. Robert had made bacon and eggs and there were warm fresh rolls, jams and marmalades, orange juice, and excellent coffee.

We skied to the lifts at 9.30. I found that Élise was an elegant skier, and that she had first skied at the age of ten. I attempted to look elegant too, and Liz rewarded me by skiing past and saying, 'looking good today.' I swelled with pride.

We took the lift to Saulire, then over to Meribel. After that I was just lost, Liz skied behind on the easy slopes correcting me, and in front on steeper ones. The others would ski a slope two or three times to my once, but I was starting to enjoy it rather than be perpetually frightened. The day was fine, the sky uniform deep blue and the snow sparkled in the strong sun. This was a really special day. At last I was appreciating the clarity of the air, the freshness upon my face and especially the thrill. Liz kept pushing me, relax your legs, she said you are not wearing heals on the runway. At first I didn't know what she meant, but it suddenly clicked and as I learned to relax, everything became less effort and my thighs no longer burned.

For lunch we had plates of soup in St. Martin de Belleville, outside on the snow in deep midwinter. Liz's boyfriend joined us and we all skied the afternoon. Simon said he was pleased with my progress. We took the easy route home, and I was relieved, my legs were tired by then and I was exhausted from trying to keep up.

Back in the chalet we had tea and another of Robert's wonderful cakes. I went up to our bedroom and fell asleep as soon as I had stripped off my ski clothing.

Simon wakened me to get ready for dinner at seven. Again we dressed smart casual, and he chose for me a cream chiffon blouse, mini skirt and holdups.

When we were all assembled, champagne and canapés were served, Gérard removing the corks with a sword that hung over the fireplace. I watched the happy couple. They looked so good together. Annette sat next to me, on the sofa and told me something of her work. The change from journalist to PR was something that she would not have contemplated a year ago, she said, but the opportunity Simon had given her had come at a time that was convenient. She and Gérard would marry in the summer. She asked me to be a bridesmaid.

'Of course, I would love to be. Thank you so much for thinking of me.' Simon smiled from across the room.

I loved this chalet. Of all the places I had been, this was the one I liked most. Partly it was the contrast between minus twenty degrees outside and seventy-five degrees inside, making one feel all the more snug. But it was more than that. Here I had only ever been amongst friends and it felt like home. Robert and his wife Jacqueline looked after us so well too.

The dinner was the best yet, all my favourites. Tuna tartare and French toast, crayfish tails and salad, my beloved duck and chocolate fondant. After that we sat in the lounge and snacked on cheese and biscuits, coffee and liqueurs.

We slept well. I awoke holding him. I stumbled from the bed, my leg muscles complaining. Getting down the stairs was difficult. I ate a minimal breakfast of cereal and orange juice. We skied all day and had excellent fun. Jean Luc whizzed around us like a bee, skiing up what appeared to be walls and jumping off banks with ease.

The next morning, we three students departed for Paris. I left Simon reluctantly. This holiday, he had been more passionate and tender, not trying tricks. It was as though we had a new understanding. Perhaps we were becoming like an old married couple rather than lovers. I did not know when I would see him again.

We resumed our studies. The winter dragged on. Paris was very cold, although of course, the apartment was warm and snug. My picture had been delivered and Jerome came in to hang it for me. I loved it. I could not wait to show Simon. He phoned two or three times a week, from all over the World. At the end of February, he announced that his new son had been born and all was well.

At last, a week before Easter, the weather lifted and the temperature soared to twenty degrees. The plain trees began to shoot along the Seine, and girls began to strip off their top layers. We students became light hearted and looked forward to our short Easter break. We took a night off and went to Willi's to drink cocktails. I woke feeling groggy and told myself never again. It would be wine from now on.

A letter from Vanessa told me that Stuart was getting married in August. Clair was going to university next

September. Ellie was embedded with the troops in Afghanistan.

I heard from Sam too. She was now enjoying Cambridge and had a boyfriend. They would both like to visit in the summer. I replied that it would be fine to come in July.

Simon had been in Paris, but had not visited. I was disappointed. The thought festered in my mind that he had tired of me. After a week of misery, I phoned Annette. We arranged to meet next day for lunch.

Annette was her usual calm and pleasant self. Her wedding was now not far away. I had yet to see the bridesmaid dress. It seemed everyone had someone except me.

'Simon hasn't been to see me,' I blurted out miserably, trying to hold back my tears. 'Have I done something wrong.'

'No I do not think it anything to do with you. He is having a very hard time with Catherine and that bitch Françoise. Françoise is making more trouble than there already was. Catherine has threatened to tell the media about you and Simon, and to sue for divorce as a result. Simon does not wish to have your name, or his all over the news again. He is particularly protective of you. Françoise is absolute poison and for some reason positively hates you.'

'But we have hardly met. Last Christmas, yes, but we only exchanged a dozen words.'

'That is enough with that one, and of course, Catherine would see you dead. That he prefers you to her, well, she is very rude about you.'

'I think I know what she would say.'

'Catherine and Françoise together, bounce off each other. One suggests a nasty scheme or a victim and the other joins in. You know the syndrome, like two bullies at school, each trying to outdo the other. I don't know how he lives there, when he is home that is. But he returns to the Château because it is his and because of the children.

'And Simon is very busy too. He has this new designer and range. He is trying to sell into multiples, so he is visiting all over Europe. I will tell him that you are worried.'

'No. Please don't. I will speak to him myself, when I am ready. Thank you Annette. Do me a favour though? If he is in real trouble, then let me know, please?

'Of course. You should not have this worry. How old are you?'

'Twenty. Twenty one in September.'

'And your studies? It's going well?'

'Oh yes. A good way of getting rid of misery is hard work. We three are all determined and, well, clever. We are the three brains of our year, and we all help each other. It works well, the three musketeers. I don't think I would still be there without them to help me, because my French, especially medical French is lacking. Everyday French, I am fine, but when it comes to pathology or oncology, I would be lost without them.'

'I'm glad you are succeeding, I know it is a very difficult course. Well I have to go. If you need me just ring. Don't brood, it is always better to meet a problem head on.'

'You once said, you were trying to get information on Françoise. Did you?'

'No. I had forgotten. Yes, I will see what I can find out. I know there is something. I believe she came from somewhere around Nantes.'

We kissed and she departed. I walked home, a little less unhappy, but still worried. I did not like Simon having this trouble and I could see no way out of it. I knew that he did brood on things, and I feared for him dashing about the continent. He was brooding when we first met, then it was about his dead sister. Damn Schûster and her lover. Why couldn't she have kept her bargain? On impulse, I phoned Simon. When he answered, I could tell he was in the car.

'Ma cherie,' 'I cannot speak now, I have a call coming from New York. I'll phone you tonight. Je suis désolé.' The phone went dead. His voice sounded strange. I almost thought I had phoned Gérard.

Chapter 15.

Catherine was dead. The call from Annette sent me reeling to the settee.

'How?'

'I don't know. I spoke to Françoise as soon as I heard. The police phoned me asking where Simon is.'

'Have you spoken to him?'

'No. He has not answered his phone. He was taking a few days off, going to the chalet. But I spoke to Robert. He has not arrived. He is not with you?'

'No. I wish he was.'

'If you hear from him, the police are trying to find him to tell him. Ask him to phone me first, would you?'

'Of course Annette.' I put down the phone unsteadily.

Élise and Jean Luc went to a lecture. I stayed by the phone.

Thirty minutes later and Madame Gameau was at the door with two men.

They showed me identification, an Inspector from the 2nd Arrondissement and his sidekick. They were of course looking for Simon. They insisted on searching the flat. I sat terrified. After their perfunctory search, they asked questions.

'When did you last see him?'

'At Christmas.'

'Where did you go?'

'To the chalet.'

'When did you last hear from him?'

'Three days ago on the phone. But I phoned him this afternoon and he was in his car on the way to Courchevel.'

'Do you know where he is now?'

'No.'

'If you hear from him, you must phone us immediately, or else it could be serious for you.'

'How did Catherine die,' I asked. They would not say.

They disappeared, saying they might be back.

I phoned Annette. She had spoken to Simon's housekeeper. Apparently, Françoise had taken the babies to the doctor, leaving Simon and Catherine alone in the Château, except for the staff in their quarters. There had been a furious row before Simon departed for Courchevel. When Françoise returned, she found Catherine unconscious at the foot of the stairs. She had died in the ambulance. It looked bad she said. I promised again to tell her if I heard from him.

I sat by the phone all day. I wanted Vanessa, but I did not dare phone in case Simon was trying to phone me. Finally I used the mobile and asked Vanessa to come over. She would arrive next morning.

I phoned Annette again. She was en route to the Château, as was Gérard, to look after things there. That left me in Paris. My friends returned. We attempted to work, but in the end we gave up. Élise cooked.

We ate, and sat about, just not knowing what to say or do. The TV news said they were searching for the Comte de Beauvonne. Fifteen minutes later, Madame Gameau came up to say that the press were continually ringing the doorbell from beyond the iron railings and gate. Annette had said meet trouble. I decided to speak to them.

By the time I reached the front gate, there were ten of them there. At first I was going to talk to them through the bars, but I thought better of it. I retreated and asked Madame to bring jugs of coffee. When all was ready, I asked them to follow me into Simon's vestibule, with Madame Gameau and Jerome standing guard to see no one wandered. I stood on the stairs. There was a buzz of expectancy. They helped themselves to coffee.

'S'il vous plait, Messieurs et Mesdames.' The buzz stopped. 'Some of you know me. I am Trudi the model and Simon de Beauvonne's protégé. I have an apartment here that I share with two other medical students. As you may know I am also a student at the Sorbonne.

'I am afraid we and the staff of the Comte know no more than you. The police have been to ask for le Comte but he is not here and has not been here for the last three months. I am sorry that we know nothing. We are all very worried for his safety and of course, devastated by the death of his wife. That is all we know and all I have to say. Now please do not keep ringing the bell. I promise that if we hear any news, we will keep you informed if we can.'

'Are you his mistress Trudi?' A voice asked from the crowd. I tried to see who it was.

'Oh if only monsieur. I am afraid the Comte de Beauvonne is far above my station and much older also. Non monsieur, he, Simon de Beauvonne is a devoted father and spends practically all his time at the Château. We communicate because he has provided me with this apartment, but I have not seen him for nearly five months. Au revoir, Mesdames et Messieurs.'

They drifted out and the gate closed behind them. Madame Gameau patted my hand. I went up the stairs and into the apartment. I was terribly worried. What had happened at the Château? Where was Simon now? I could not think to do anything until I knew where he was.

Vanessa arrived at 2 am. John had driven her to London and she had caught the first train available from Stratford. I hugged her as though she was my own long lost mother, then tears and sobs could no longer be held back.

We went to bed almost immediately, having just briefly filled her in with the sketchy details as far as I knew them. By six I was up and sitting nervously by the phones. Vanessa slept on. Jean Luc and Elise were on the move by seven. Jean Luc kissed my head. Élise asked if I would like them to stay with me.

'No Élise, I need you to go to la Pitié to keep me up to date. If I hear anything I will text you. Vanessa is here, so I am not alone.'

Vanessa rose at 9 am and ordered me to dress and do my face. I did so like an obedient child, choosing slacks and my best silk blouse.

It was almost 11.30 when Annette rang. Simon had been found. His car, with him still in it, had been at the bottom of a ravine near Clermont Ferrand. He was now in hospital there. I sent a text to Élise, asking her to relay any messages for me when they returned.

I decided to drive to Clermont. Vanessa agreed to hire a car and bring it to the rear entrance. It was nearly one by the time we set off for the four-hour drive. We had avoided the reporters by leaving by the little used rear entrance. The small BMW buzzed along happily, but my stomach was in turmoil. I displayed impatience with a driver, and Vanessa told me to calm down.

We arrived at the hospital Gabriel Montpied, a mile outside the city of Clermont Ferrand, after five and were directed to a waiting room. We sat waiting for over thirty minutes, until a surgeon appeared in a green gown, his mask pulled down.

'You are the relatives of Simon de Beauvonne?'

'Yes.'

'He is still in surgery. He was very badly injured and he was not discovered for over twelve hours. He has lost blood and we had to amputate his right leg below the knee, to release him from the vehicle and because there was gangrene. He is very ill indeed. He also has some chest injuries and superficial cuts to his face. We are most concerned about spinal damage. He has feeling in his legs but he has two fractured vertebrae. It is very serious. I would advise you to go to a hotel, make yourselves comfortable and come back in the morning. You can phone the hospital at any time and ask for the latest news. The police are also here. They wish to speak to him regarding the death of his wife.'

'Will he recover?'

'Until he regains consciousness, we will not know and then how much? But we hope. Now I must attend my patient. I will know more tomorrow, when we have tidied him up.'

We left and found a hotel. We went to dinner, but I could not eat. In the bedroom Vanessa gave me a pill to take and like a child I swallowed it obediently. I thought I would not sleep, but I did. I had erotic dreams of Simon, inexplicable considering the state of my mind, but when I told Vanessa, she said it was the effects of the sleeping pill.

I rang the hospital. Simon was in the Critical Care Unit, still unconscious. We were there within half an hour.

A policeman sat outside and asked for my name, which he wrote in a register. A priest asked if I would like him to pray? Do what you like, I said, is that not what you are paid for?

Vanessa sat outside while I went in to sit beside him. A nurse was busy, checking drips, monitoring instruments. I watched the heart monitor bleeping regularly, the trace rippling across the screen. There seemed to be pipes in every orifice. The respiratory balloon inflated and deflated. The room buzzed with machinery. After half an hour of holding a limp hand, I went out to Vanessa. I texted everyone with an update. The press turned up half an hour later. I had nothing to tell them.

All that day, I sat beside him, hoping for an awakening, a flicker of sentient life, but there was none. At 9 pm, Vanessa ordered that we return to the hotel, saying that the hospital would inform us of any change. The same pattern followed over the next three days, the newspapers became full of speculation that there had been a fight and during it, Catherine had fallen down the stairs. The police had made no accusation. They said that as a matter of course they wanted to interview Simon, to see whether he could throw any light on what had occurred in the Château.

They also wanted to find out how Simon had crashed off the road and into the ravine.

I was asked once again if I knew anything, and of course I didn't. I don't think they believed me. I didn't care. I just wanted Simon to wake up.

It was Friday. I had now been in Clermont Ferrand four days. The nurses and the doctors had encouraged me to talk to Simon, even though there was no response. On impulse, I asked for the screens to be brought round the bed. At first they would not agree. I had to make the nurse aware of the intimate nature of what I was going to do. It was embarrassing, but if it worked it would be worth it. Talking to him all the time, I bared a breast and placed his hand upon it. Nothing, no response. I bit his ear and whispered, 'feel my posy.' I took his hand and guided him. I was rewarded with just a flutter of his eyelids. I leant over the bed and kissed him on the lips and this time, he let out a sigh. For the next hour I kept up a steady conversation, about us, nothing about the Château or Catherine, not even the House of Beauvonne. Again I bit his ear and nuzzled his neck. I felt round his stomach and grasped his hip. This time his eyes flickered, then opened. He tried to speak but the respirator tube in his throat would not allow him to. I motioned him to be silent, putting my finger to my lips. I rang for the nurse. When she came and saw that he was at last awake, she sent for the doctor. They asked me to leave.

Vanessa and I clung to each other for what seemed an age. When my sobs of relief subsided, I released myself and sat. Vanessa, was resourceful as always and soon cups of coffee were provided. I sat on the edge of my chair, tense, hoping that he would wake with his mind whole even if his body wasn't. I wanted to pace, but Vanessa held my hand and kept me seated.

After what seemed an unreasonable length of time, the doctor opened the door and beckoned me in. 'You brought him round, now he needs your support. You have to tell him of the loss of his leg, but not today unless he asks. You will also have to speak about the death of his wife, but be gentle, careful how you tell him. Perhaps ask him what he remembers. Again, not today if possible. You can do this?'

'Yes of course. I am a student médicin at the Sorbonne, so I understand perfectly.'

'Good. We have removed the respirator, but he still has the other tubes. Apart from his amputation, his damage seems to be superficial, although his back may give him trouble in future years. He will have to remain here for perhaps six weeks, while the fractured vertebrae mend, but I am hopeful that he makes a good recovery. One more thing. I have to write a report for the police. I shall try to paint a less optimistic picture so that he is not disturbed. I am not allowing them to interview him at the moment. Bon chance Trudi.'

I entered the CCU. He recognised me immediately, for he gave a wan smile. I kissed his forehead and took his hand in mine.

'Trudi,' he whispered hoarsely, 'I do not understand what happened. Why am I here? They say this is Clermont Ferrand?'

'Do you remember nothing?'

'I was going to the Chalet. I needed to get away from everything for a few days. That is all I remember.'

'So you were at the Château and you were driving to Courchevel, just as we have before. What happened?'

'I don't know Trudi. I can't remember. I was driving, then I wake up here. How long have I been here?'

'Nearly five days. You have been unconscious. You have broken vertebrae in your lower back from the crash.

That is why you are immobile. They are cooling that area to reduce any swelling which could occur and which might damage your spinal cord. They are also keeping you stretched. It is imperative that you remain tranquil. You understand?'

'Yes Trudi. How long will I be here?'

'Until they are satisfied that you are mended enough to put weight on your spine. You drove the car off a precipice. They did not find you for sixteen hours. There is something else.'

I took his hand in mine. 'You were still strapped in the car when they found you.'

'How is the car?'

'Never mind the car. It does not matter but it will not be driven again. It is you I worry about. Sometimes in a bad accident, people are trapped, often by a foot or by both feet. In your case, it was one foot. To save you, they had to cut.......'

'The car?'

'No, salaud the car. You, they had to cut you.'

'Where? Not,,,,,,,,,?' He tried to point to his crutch.

'No, Simon. It is your left leg. To free you from the wreckage. You were very weak and suffering from exposure. They had to get you out quickly. You have lost your leg, below the knee. I am sorry. They asked me to tell you.'

'Does Catherine know?' Is she here?'

'No Simon, she is not here. I will explain tomorrow. I am here with Vanessa.'

'So I only have one foot.?'

'Oui, mon homme chéri. But they say, they can give you a false one, and you will still be able to ski and walk and ride your horses. You will, chéri, still be good in bed.'

'So!' He was quiet for a few seconds. 'I would like to be skiing with you now. And you? You should be at University.'

'Élise and Jean Luc are emailing me the work, so I can keep up on computer in the hotel.'

'So how long must I be here?'

'We don't know. At the moment it is too soon to move you.'

'Thank you, for telling me. It is a lot for a young woman to have to do.'

'You have done so much for me. I do this not to repay that, but because I love you Simon. It is for me to care for you, while you are injured. Then you can look after me again. Teach me how to be a refined lady.'

'Do you not know, you are that already Trudi.'

'You must be a good teacher then. How am I going to wait weeks for you to make love to me again? You must get plenty of rest and be a good patient. You are tired, Simon dear. I will leave you. I will come back tomorrow morning. Rest, and get well.' I kissed him. I could see that he was already tired, and his eyes fluttered as I left. I had not dealt with the Catherine story, but that would keep for tomorrow, when I hoped he would be a little stronger.

Vanessa and I went to the hotel. Before dinner I worked on the emails from Élise and emailed back some questions on it.

Chapter 16.

Over the next two days, Simon gradually improved. Then came the moment for me to tell him about Catherine.

'Simon, I have something very important to tell you. The day you were driving to the Chalet, there was an accident at the Château. Catherine fell down the staircase.'

'Why have you not told me before?'

'Because I did not think you strong enough. I have to tell you now, because the police want to ask you some questions.'

'The police?'

'Simon, I have to tell you that Catherine died on the way to hospital.'

'No it can't be.....How could she fall?'

'Simon it is worse. Your housekeeper says that you and Catherine had a fearful row that day. That is why they want to speak to you. They came to Paris, searched the apartment in case you were there. Then the newspapers turned up and I told them no one knew where you were. It was true. We were all worried for you. That is when I asked Vanessa to come over. The next morning you were found in the ravine by a shepherd still strapped in. I am sorry to give you such bad news.'

I grasped his hand in mine. He squeezed it.

'How could you have the burden of all this on your young shoulders? Poor Catherine, it was a bad end.' He was silent for a time. He lifted my hand and kissed my fingertips. 'Dearest Trudi, do not worry? I am sure it will all be alright.'

'Annette and Gérard are at the Château, making sure the children are safe and looked after. I have spoken to Annette and all is well, they are still in the care of Françoise. Annette is looking for another nanny to replace her and is going to Paris to interview them and also to control PR from there. Is there anything else to do? What about Maison Beauvonne? Will it run itself? Is there anything else I should be doing?'

'Ma Chere, you have done well. You have such strength and judgement. I would like you to be here when the police interview me. You must also contact my lawyer, for I will make no statement without legal advice.' He told me the name, Avocat Millet. 'He is in my mobile phone if you have my things. Send for him immediately. Then I want you to go to Paris after the police interview and speak to the Beauvonne staff. Let them know what is happening.

'After that, I want to be moved as soon as possible to the Paris house, then you must get back to work at the university. We will have a nurse to look after me so that you can work. No argument. The university is most important. Now speak to Millet and get him here for tomorrow, then we can get this police interview over. Do it now Trudi.'

I managed by cajoling, to arrange for Millet to come to Clermont Ferrand tomorrow, Monday. Then I informed the police that Simon would speak to them tomorrow in the presence of his lawyer and me.

I spoke to the doctors. They thought that a move to Paris for Simon would be possible at the end of the week, provided that a new scan showed improvement. I phoned Annette and she confirmed that Françoise was gone replaced by Sophie Maynard. I said that I was coming to Paris Tuesday and we ought to meet. We arranged to have dinner together. Gérard was staying at the Château to make sure the children were safe.

I told Simon what had been done, then I collected Vanessa and we returned to the hotel. I went to bed early and slept till seven-thirty next day. The meeting with the police was timed for midday. Millet promised to be with Simon by 11.00. I would leave for Paris on the 13.25 to Gare de Lyon, Bercy. I would be home by 17.30, time enough to freshen up to see Annette. Vanessa would stay in Clermont Ferrand with the car.

Two officers, an Inspector Corton and a detective, Avocat Millet and I assembled around Simon's bed at noon. The police asked questions, some of which Simon could not answer. He could not remember what time he had left the Château nor could he remember an argument. All in all, the interview proved nothing for Simon. He had no means of proving what time he left the Château, he could not remember the crash either. It did not look good.

I kissed him goodbye and Vanessa ran me to the station. I was just in time for the train and was soon speeding north to Paris, watching the empty French landscape whizz past. I was preoccupied with Simon's interview. I could understand his lack of memory of any happenings of that day, but if the police decided to call Catherine's death suspicious, then he would be suspect number one unless he had an alibi.

On the train I spent time thinking about Maison Beauvonne and what I would say. There were decisions to make and it seemed to me, to need a big shake up.

I took a taxi from Bercy. Élise and Jean Luc welcomed me home. I was mentally exhausted and answered their questions regarding Simon tersely. I just wanted to sleep but first I had to get myself spruced up to meet Annette.

I left the apartment at 7.00 pm and found that the press had already sensed my return. I gave an impromptu press conference, merely saying that Simon was still critical in hospital and the police had interviewed him. He had no knowledge of the accident.

They started to follow me. By chance I managed to hail a passing taxi and leave them behind. It was all becoming a nightmare and I was almost in tears by the time I entered Chez Gaston. Annette had thoughtfully booked a private room. We embraced. Something had occurred to me on the way. The clock in Simon's car would have stopped at the time of the crash surely. That might be important. I emailed Millet and Vanessa, asking them to go to the police and request inspection of the wrecked Mercedes and to witness and ask the police to witness the registered time.

Annette was her usual calm self. She said that all was well at the Château under the watchful eye of Gérard and the new nanny seemed to have care of the children under control. Françoise was not happy at losing her lover and her job, but Annette said, she had found out that Françoise possessed a criminal record, for grievous bodily harm in a fight in Nantes when she was nineteen. She had hit another girl with a bottle causing the victim a lasting disability. Dismissal therefore was easy.

I told Annette that Simon had requested I speak to all the staff, reassuring them that he was recovering and that he would soon be back in control of Maison Beauvonne. Annette would compose a press release immediately and hold a news conference when Simon was brought to Paris. Everything was therefore under control for the moment. We had done all we could. I toyed with the starter, then feeling relieved at unburdening to Annette and feeling her strength I managed to eat the main course without feeling nauseous. I returned to the apartment at 10 pm. Élise came through to see how I was. This time I could embrace her. I thanked them for all their help and said that I hoped to get back to university with them next week.

I took another of Vanessa's sleeping pills and slept long, waking to find the apartment deserted. I had slept over twelve hours. The meeting at Maison Beauvonne was for 3 pm. I washed and dressed my hair, just leaving it straight, did my makeup and dressed carefully in a deep purple silk shantung suit, smart and business like. I rehearsed my speech before the mirror, trying to get the French exactly correct and to give it the right French intonation. I did not want to appear as the little English.

At last I was satisfied. I ate an apple and some cheese, and called a taxi. Surprisingly there were no journalists about.

I arrived at quarter to three and went to Jacgues Paquet, the haute couture designer. He called in Thomas Martin, the new English ready made designer. I told them the basic message, and they gathered all the staff, crammed into the salon that had been closed to the public for an hour.

I stood on a dais which usually held a mannequin.

'I think most of you know me, Trudi, Simon de Beauvonne's protégé and part time model. I have come from Clermont Ferrand to give you a message from Simon. I am not taking control, you have your two designers for that. I am merely the messenger.

'He has been seriously ill, trapped in the car for sixteen hours before he was found by a shepherd. He has two fractured vertebrae and they amputated one leg. He was also in a coma for five days. Now he is making good progress, but is saddened by the death of his wife Catherine, who is the mother of his three children. However, it is impossible to know when he will be able to see you all again.

'He has asked me to keep you informed of his progress and to thank you for your good wishes and for the work you are doing. He may be injured but his thoughts are very much with you and he wishes you all to know that he appreciates the work you are doing to keep Beauvonne at the forefront of the fashion business. Thank you so much. I want to assure you that there are big changes to come to Beauvonne that will benefit you all.'

I shook hands with those I knew and one or two I didn't. I had a coffee with the designers who assured me that everything was under control and on time for the summer shows. I could go home and rest.

Chapter 17.

Élise and Jean Luc were home before me. I suggested that we work for two hours then I would treat them to a meal at Franco's, the Italian restaurant just a couple of blocks away. I already had quite a lot of catching up to do, even though I had worked every night in Clermont Ferrand. However, when we got down to comparing notes, I found that it was not as bad as I thought. At seven, we packed up. I phoned the hospital and they gave an optimistic report on Simon. I then spoke to Vanessa who confirmed that he was very optimistic. I told her that I had informed the staff of his progress and that all was well.

She said that the police had allowed them to look at the wrecked car, but as the clock was electronic, they could not read the time without power. The police technician said that they would extract the clock and attempt to power it up, but that it might go into self-correct mode from the atomic clock, so they would be ready to photograph the dial. Simon was out of CCU and into a private room. The press had apparently abandoned me and were now camped out at the hospital.

I was satisfied that I had done everything I could. I showered and dressed in a clean mini and top and we set off for the restaurant. Jean Luc walked between us, and arm in arm we soon covered the short distance to Franco's. It was a relief to be back with my friends and out with young people of my age.

Franco was a swarthy man, an Italian from the deep southern tip of Italy. It was rumoured that he had been in the Mafia, but lived in France banished for some misdemeanour. I had never found him anything but charming, a flatterer who gave compliments to women in such a jokey way that no one took offence. Tonight he was all solicitous, asking after Monsieur le Comte and putting a hand on my shoulder and looking directly into my face. Bella, più bella, he said as he put down the menus, then caressed Élise's shoulder. He wagged his finger at Jean Luc and said, 'You are a very lucky man, eh? Two such beauties.'

We all laughed. We selected antipasti, then various pasta dishes and some sparkling wine, which Franco said, was better than champagne. It was OK, but certainly better than some. I told them about Simon and his injuries and what I had been doing. Suddenly emotions caught up with me and I began to sob, uncontrollably. The dull lights of the restaurant shimmered in my tears and I snuffled into my napkin. Franco, ever observant, came to the table, motioned to Élise to assist me to the rear of the restaurant to his own sitting room where he shooed out his children to make room for me. All I could say, was, 'They cut off his leg.' That seemed to be the pinnacle of my distress, and I repeated it, my throat so tight that my voice had risen to a quiet scream. Élise cuddled me in my sudden distress, and Franco reappeared with a glass of cognac.

'Drink,' he said and like a child I obeyed, pouring the fiery liquid that I never touched normally, down my throat. Whether it was the jolt of alcohol or the burning in my throat,

I was shocked out of my tears. I looked in the mirror and wiped the tears. We returned to the table. Our food was replaced with fresh plates. I apologised to my friends. Jean Luc told me of some funny incidents at the hospital and I eventually managed a laugh.

Franco wanted to waive the bill but I insisted on paying. I thanked him and his sweet stout wife who was very motherly towards me. We all kissed and we returned to the apartment.

I went straight to bed, taking another sleeping pill. I woke once in the night but went back to sleep immediately. Morning came too soon.

At the university there was a message to see Professor Rousse, who had admonished me for doing modelling. I found him in his office. He was a florid man, of around fifty years old. He was known to be outspoken, a martinet and intolerant of any student he thought was a time waster.

'So Trudi Nash, our celebrity student, you honour us with your presence again. What is it this time that was more important than lectures?'

'Monsieur le Comte is in hospital, professor. He was in a coma and I had to take care of him. Also his wife has died in an accident, so I could not do otherwise than go to him.' I could not believe that he was not aware.

'Oh Mademoiselle, I had not realised that he was your guardian? Why did you not tell me?'

'I thought everyone knew.'

'The student tittle-tattle does not reach me, and I confess that I seldom read or listen to the celebrity news. So, how is Le Comte.'

'They have had to amputate his leg below the knee and he has two hair line cracks in his vertebrae.' Tears filled my eyes but I managed some control.

'Ma pauvre. Mademoiselle Trudi. Is he progressing?'

'Oui maître. He was in a coma for five days, but I managed to bring him out of it by talking and caressing him.'

'And you are really serious about being un médicin?'

'Oui maître, and le Comte sent me home because he said my studies were most important. I hope that he will be brought to Paris as soon as it is safe.'

'I have not been fair to you. Perhaps I was dazzled by beauty, and thought no one with those looks could also be serious. I will make a note, not to be so judgemental. If I can help your studies, to give extra coaching, then you must come to me. My door is open to you. Now thank you for coming. Join your companions.'

I found it hard getting back into study that morning. My mind was really two hundred miles away in Clermont Ferrand. By the afternoon I felt more like a student again. I could not wait though, to phone and speak to Simon.

Vanessa phoned just as I emerged from Opera station. 'The police are charging Simon with Catherine's murder. Apparently they have a statement from Françoise and another from the housekeeper, that there was a furious argument between Catherine and Simon.'

'Do they have physical evidence that he caused her to fall down the stairs?'

'No, I don't think so '

'So there was no witness to her fall?'

'No. The housekeeper thought she heard the row. Françoise had of course gone to the doctor with the children but she says they were always at loggerheads. Simon says that he left the Château a full hour before Catherine was discovered. It is proving that which is difficult.'

'And the car clock, does not tell us when he crashed?'

'No the police say the clock cannot be revived.'

'That's not good. Did he stop anywhere on route?'

'He says not.'

'I need time to think Vanessa. There must be something. I'll talk to you tomorrow. Give him my love and say I will phone him. I need time to think. There must be way. The media will love this.'

I pocketed my phone and let myself into the apartment. Jean Luc and Élise arrived thirty minutes later. We made dinner early so we could work and go straight to bed afterwards. I told them of the charge,

'So it is all about timing,' Jean Luc said, 'if Simon was not there then it would have to be an accident. There must be someone who saw his car.'

Next morning the TV and the newspapers were full of it. Outside there were a dozen reporters. I pushed through them with Jean Luc's help. They shouted questions. Exhausted I turned on them.

'It is all a mistake. Le Comte de Beauvonne had left long before his wife was discovered injured, and we shall prove it. That is all I have to say.'

We made our way to Pitié. The newspapers were awful. My parents phoned, worried that I was involved. It could not be worse. Somehow I dragged myself from lecture to lecture. The good news came that evening, that Simon could be moved to Paris to be looked after in his own house, but a policeman would be present all the time. Annette arranged for a live in nurse, experienced in back injuries. I would be able to see him everyday.

By the evening, the papers had resurrected Simon's sponsorship of me and photos of my crash on the catwalk. They also hinted that Simon's marriage had been in trouble. The article in particular from Elizabeth Dufour was full of innuendo.

I phoned Annette. She was she said, aware, but there was little she could do other than issue refutation stories, which she had done and which would appear next day. However, she suspected that some of this was coming from the sacked Françoise, and Millet had issued an injunction on her disclosure of family information on behalf of the children.

I wondered whether we should admit the marriage was in trouble and cite the liaison with Françoise, but then that might provide a motive for Catherine's murder. I talked about it with Annette and we decided to keep quiet and wait to see what transpired. So far the police had not asked us about the state of the marriage. In any case, I really knew nothing except hearsay. Catherine had showed me distain but I had not witnessed a row between her and Simon.

Simon would arrive home tomorrow by ambulance, the hired nurse travelling with him. The policeman would arrive at 14.00 and would be stationed in the vestibule.

Chapter 18.

Arrival day dawned bright and sunny, but with a cold wind blowing out of the east. We walked in silence to the Opera metro. I had decided to go to Uni in the morning and go home to welcome Simon at lunch time. Madame Gameau had prepared his room and filled it with flowers from the market on Ile de la Cité. A special bed had been substituted for his four poster. That itself had involved specialists to take down and move the heavy old bed where we had first made love.

The morning passed quickly with a lecture on pathology and we even had time to write it up and test each other in the café. I left and made my way quickly home. Simon had not arrived before me. I asked Madame Gameau to tell me as soon as he arrived.

He arrived at three thirty. He looked so much better than a week ago. I hovered until he was finally installed, then I was at last able to have some time alone with him.

'So, now you are not in control as you like to be. If I put my head under the blanket, are you going to tell me off?'

'You devil. I am defenceless and you would attack me? What kind of doctor will you be?'

'But seriously, how are you? If there is anything I can do, I mean anything, you know I will.'

'No. Not yet. Perhaps in a day or two. So how are your friends? You are all working at your studies? Have you caught up after your week in Clermont?'

'Yes I think so. They have been very good to me, kept notes and handouts, but it is never as good as being there. Professor Rousse had me in to tell me off about my absence, but when he knew where I had been, he offered extra coaching. Maybe I will accept.'

'And you. You have enough money. Your allowance is enough?'

'Oui. I am fine. I have enough.'

'Good. I have been thinking about Jean Luc. He is a good boy, yes?'

'Ah oui. He is lovely, but his parents are quite poor, and their life hard.'

'I know. I have a position on the estate that his father might suit and perhaps his mother could also work in the Château. I would like you to bring him to me, so I can gauge his reaction, perhaps when he comes from university?'

'Of course. It is good of you. But he is a ski instructeur in winter. Could he still do that?'

'I have the grand plan. While I lay there, I worked it all out if they agree. His father could keep the roads of the estate in summer. In winter he could use the servants quarters in the chalet. Robert does not use them, he has his own place. He would also be on hand to guide us and our guests and business contacts, and when not doing that, he could teach private clients. What do you think?'

'He would have security? When he gets old? I presume he would have a cottage on the estate. Would that be for life?'

'Of course. I have three spare cottages at the moment. It is not a problem.'

'Then I suggest you ask Jean Luc.'

I sent Jean Luc to him when he returned. They were together some time. Jean Luc returned beaming. That evening he phoned his father. He wanted time to think about the offer, he said. Moving from Haute Savoie and all their friends to flat Normandy with no friends would be a wrench. On the other hand, Jean Luc said, the salary offered and the freedom in winter, with free accommodation for life, was attractive.

Jean Luc also mentioned that Simon was worried about proving he was absent when the accident to Catherine occurred. Something Jean Luc had read about, he told me was that position could be proved from mobile phone calls.

I phoned Annette.

'The mobile,' I said, 'Annette, I phoned Simon that afternoon. He also said he was expecting a call from New York.'

'You are sure?'

'Yes. Positive. That day is printed on my mind. I remember every moment. How could I forget?'

'If you are sure, then I will get a private investigator on to it. But you really are sure?'

'Of course Annette. He was in the car, I could hear the road noise and it was poor reception.'

'I will make enquiries straight away. This could be really important. I now seem to remember reading about this in the news. I'll let you know what happens. Au revoir.' She was always so calm. No wonder Simon had made her his PR guru.

I said nothing to Simon. Later in the evening I met the nurse, a nice girl from Lyon, very experienced. She thought that Simon would soon be up and about. His leg had healed well and the latest spinal scans also looked good. There was minimal bruising. He would start exercises in a few days. The minor lacerations to his hands and face from windscreen glass had more or less disappeared.

'So when will they give him a new leg.'

'Perhaps in three months. We need to wait for the stump to fully heal and all the swelling go and the nerves to settle down. Then I think with practise, no one will ever know he has an artificial leg.'

The word stump cut through me. I restrained a shudder.

'He will ride a horse and ski?'

'If he wants to enough, he will. It is really up to him.'

I was satisfied that he was in good hands and the outlook was bright.

The rest of the week I was a student full time, feeling much happier. On Friday evening, I phoned Annette about the mobile phone records. It was reassuring. When Catherine was found, Simon was a hundred and ten miles away, at least two hours driving time, according to the records obtained from the mobile provider. It was a relief.

'Now, we are waiting for the police to examine the records. They have to believe them. The phone was in his car when his body was discovered. So it looks good. Catherine I suspect, was in a bad temper and slipped on the marble stair case. Then she slid all the way to the bottom. A tragedy.'

'What about the evidence from the housekeeper?'

'She now says that she could have been mistaken. The radio was on upstairs when Catherine was discovered, so it could have been that she heard. In any case, we had her hearing tested and it is only about fifty per cent. Gérard says that the babies are all fine.

'Now, what about you? How is your work going? You have exams this year?'

'Yes. Pathology, histology, the pulmonary system, biophysics, anatomy. We should all be OK. We are all bright, and we make a good team. I am very lucky to have such friends.'

'Good Trudi. Look after Simon. He needs you more than ever now. And study hard too. I will let you know as soon as I have a decision from the police. Then I will see to that salope Dufour. I am going to sue for €5 million. Au revoir.'

It was not a few days before Simon was up and about, but three weeks, just to be quite sure, the doctors said. If he wanted to ride again and to ski, they had to make sure everything healed correctly.

The policeman had been withdrawn a week after I spoke to Annette. The papers came out with a different story. Now it was all a tragic accident, and a family that was cursed. They revived the death of his sister and his parents relatively early demise. They even published a history of the family, from escaping the guillotine to restoration under Napoleon III. However it was too late for Dufour. Millet had slapped a suit for damages on behalf of the family and me, not for €5 million, but for ten.

The world started to look good again. Summer had come to Paris. Girls were in skimpy tops, not as bereft of clothing as girls in London, but pretty in sweet frocks, skirts and sleeveless tops and lightweight slacks, looking cool and chic. Men opened their shirt necks and carried summer jackets slung over a nonchalant shoulder.

Exam time came and went. It was not easy, but it was OK, we all agreed. We compared answers afterwards and celebrated with a lunch at a fashionable lunch venue, Willi's Wine bar, Rue des Petits Champs. Simon managed to meet us there, skipping along on crutches. It was super gay in the traditional meaning of the word, with young and old, fashionable people. We ate well off the lunch menu but Simon lashed out on the champagne. Today he said, Dufour and her paper had offered a settlement of €4 million, and he had accepted. He was also taking us all to dinner on the Bateaux Mouches. It was dress up time tonight before Élise and Jean Luc departed tomorrow.

Simon came through to the apartment, the first time since the accident. He looked in my wardrobe with Élise and selected a strapless ruby gown for her which I had never worn. She just managed to squeeze into it. It looked good on her though.

When Élise had gone, he turned his attention to me. I still had dresses I had never worn, and every visit Simon made, he seemed to bring another outfit for me. This time it was an emerald sheath dress, just above the knee, with a short split in the back. I said I never wore green, but Simon maintained that I should. The bodice was boned and self-supporting, so there was no need for a brassiere. He selected black silk string pants, but then suggested that I wear none.

'Why?' I asked.

'Because I like to think of you vulnerable, your posy for all to see beneath the dress. No one will know except me.'

'Very well Simon. As this is our first outing together since your accident and Catherine's death, but I like to wear pants. This once only.'

He shrugged. 'Your smokey eyes, tonight please Cherie, for me.'

He left and I went about my toilet. For some reason the knickers thing bothered me. I wanted to be above all respectable in public. What I did with a lover in private was another matter, but this seemed an invasion of my privacy. I was vulnerable enough. Maybe he had just caught me in a mood, but I had a feeling of oppression. By the time I had run the straighteners through my hair and done my makeup, I had thrown off the feeling and was more secure. I wore the string pants. The sheath really hugged my figure, fitted beautifully with no bulges. Jean Luc sitting dressed in the salon zipped me up.

'You are a beautiful creature, Trudi. I mean it. When I look at you I can hardly believe that you are human. You look out of this World and I wonder what we are doing here with you.'

'Don't be silly Jean Luc. I am a poor thing. Élise is a wonderful person and you Jean Luc, are my only male friend. I value you both above all. This exterior pleases me, but I envy you and Élise. Really. The package, what you see, hides imperfections.'

'Of course I love Élise, but she, I know and understand. When she takes time and bothers with her makeup, she is very beautiful to me, but she is still my fiancée. You on the other hand are...an ideal. You may have something missing, like a womb, but so do some natal females. I will not hear you say you are imperfect. You are....'

'Ethereal is the word, I think Jean Luc.' Simon had entered the room. 'Oui, c'est vrai. Incidentally, Jean Luc, your father has agreed to come and work for me. I am readying the house for them. He drives a hard bargain, but I am pleased. I would like if you and Élise would come and stay at the Château this summer for a week. It would be company for Trudi and we could have some nice times together.'

'I will ask her Simon. Thank you it sounds delightful.'

Élise appeared, looking really more beautiful than I had ever seen her. I watched as Jean Luc took a deep breath and I smiled at the effect a beautiful female could have on a male. We are after all, just another animal on this small planet.

We took a taxi to the Pont d'Alma. On board I was surprised to find not only Vanessa and John but also Ellie. I had not seen John for over two years. I was surprised when he kissed me. 'Well, look at you,' he said.

I dragged Simon aside. 'There are no more surprises are there. I mean, you are not proposing or anything in front of these people. Simon, be truthful with me.'

'You don't want me to?'

'So you were. No not here. If you are to ask me, then it must be a private thing between us. And not yet. It is too soon after Catherine's death. The newspapers would have a fine time, and all the whispers would start again. No, I forbid it and would refuse, much as I love you, and you know I do. But this is not the way. We show respect to Catherine, however bad you found her. We are personalities. We would be crucified by the press.'

'OK, but secretly?'

'Perhaps. I will think about it. Simon, you know it is what I desire most, but I have my studies, we have our careers and reputations. Catherine has only been dead four months. No it will not do. Meanwhile I will be your companion and lover in private, we can manage that. And I very much want to be involved with your children. I am so looking forward to seeing them this summer. So please, be patient.'

His hand had wandered to my derriere.

'So you wore pants after all. You are becoming very independent. Very well, as you wish.' He kissed me. 'But I must spend more time at the Château with the children, or they will think that Gérard is their father, and I want you to be there when you can. I want you to promise.'

'Of course.' I said readily.

He led me back to our guests still sipping Champagne.

'Now everybody, I want to say a few words,' he said and his voice echoed around the boat on the PA system. 'This girl,' he raised my hand, 'saved my life. She almost made love to me, while I was in a coma, and that brought me round, I can tell you. Yes, the nurse told me how devoted you were. As a token to say thank you, there is something for you to see.' He signalled to the Maitre d'. A searchlight lit the tow path. 'That is my surprise for you Trudi, with my eternal thanks for giving me life,' he said.

We all followed the beam cutting through the dusk. On the tow path was a Mercedes SLK tourer, hood down, gleaming in silver grey, a wide pink ribbon and bow around it.

I felt such a fool for doubting him and his judgement.

The whole boat erupted with applause. I then realised that the other guests were Maison Beauvonne staff. I blushed. I did a little curtsey, to him then kissed him on the cheek, four times. Then we seated ourselves. He had provided all my favourites, baked spider crab, followed by gazpacho. Then we drew breath and chattered, before a beef wellington appeared, rare, with sauté potatoes and spinach and a red wine sauce. The sweet was strawberries and ice cream or cream. Coffee and ligueurs followed at our leisure as Paris passed before us, the bridges lit also Le Tour Eiffel, Notre Dame. It was a magical setting.

When we returned to the quay, a line of taxis was ready to take people home. My Mercedes was waiting for me, a pair of scissors provided to cut the ribbon, and Simon and I, with Élise and Jean Luc, drove at Simon's direction, around Paris, round the Arc de Triomphe and down the Champs Élysées. and home. Jean Luc helped Simon to the lift and to my room but we did not make love. He was quite exhausted. I just cuddled him. His stump disturbed me at first, then I thought about it logically. It did not matter.

Next day my friends departed, first to Jean Luc's home in Bourg, then to her parents in Normandy. They would join us at the Château in two weeks time. Simon, with my help, spent some time at Maison Beauvonne over the next two days. At last we departed for the Château, driving in my new car. I felt like a princess but luckier.

Chapter 19.

I found Annette and Gérard were still at the Château. I was glad to see them there, my good friends. I was put in a different room, adjacent to Simon's. It was beautiful, pale blue and white, a four poster bed with golden posts and gossamer silk curtains embroidered with poppies and cornflowers. In the wardrobe I found all sorts of goodies, including riding wear, the finest riding boots and a silver tipped whip. Once again the bathroom was ancient but it all worked.

I went to the nursery and introduced myself to Sophie Maynard. I liked her immediately. I was given baby Sébastien to change and found that it was nothing to be horrified by. We squatted on the floor and amused the twins,

André and Adèle, tickling them and watching as they made tiny unsteady steps between us.

Simon appeared and sat watching as we played. He had not met Sophie before either. I asked Simon in English if she could join us for dinner, and he said of course.

We went down to the salon to find a message from the artificial limb maker in England. Simon had employed them to make the prosthetic because due to the war in Afghanistan, they were European leaders in making them. They had sent over a specialist to take casts and find out Simon's requirement, but now he had to go to have it fitted and adjusted if necessary. It meant a week in England, not particularly what I wanted to do at the moment, but I would be able to see my family and perhaps visit Sam.

We stayed in the Château another couple of days. I spent a morning on horseback, chased around the paddock on a long rein by the groom, Sabine, under Simon's critical eye. He made me dress in the full kit, and I have to say, I revelled in it. It was incredibly hard work and I felt I would never be able to walk properly again when I finally dismounted. Simon said my posture had improved at least, and I had the rhythm of the trot. I said I would need a lot more practice. 'Three hours a day for a month, and you will be something like on a well-behaved horse. You have the right mount in Sheba, the little Arab mare, you just need the time and application. When I have my leg, then we can ride all day.

We drove to Dieppe and took the ferry for Newhaven, the same ferry Sam and I had used on the way out twenty-one months ago. So much had happened since then. I so enjoyed the Mercedes, cruising through Sussex and into London to the prosthetics specialist.

They were soon fitting it to Simon's stump. Then he made tentative steps between balance bars, learning how to flick it forward. He was disappointed that his walk looked strange, but the specialist said that with practice, no one would know eventually. After an hour, they were satisfied that he was walking adequately with two sticks, at least better than with the crutches. I drove us to my parents.

Father met us at the door and I was surprised when he clasped Simon to his bosom in a very un-British way. He hugged and kissed me as though I was a long lost child. Mother came to the door, wiping her hands on her apron, which she then quickly discarded. She kissed Simon, asking after his health and then me, tears filling her eyes.

'Shush,' I said, 'I am here now, all in one piece. We are fine. How are you?'

'Oh we rub along,' she said. 'I worry about you and of course your brother. He is expected back from Afghanistan in four weeks, then going on a course at Sandhurst, so hopefully, he will have seen the last of Afghanistan. It is hard, having both my son and daughter so far away.

'Anyway, I have cooked a meal and it will be ready in half an hour if you want to freshen up. Father will take you up to your rooms.'

'One room mummy. I will sleep with Simon.'

'Oh well, whatever you young things want to do. I'm old fashioned I expect, but it is not so much of a shock.'

I helped Simon negotiate the stairs.

I freshened up. I told Simon that I would go down and help mother. I found her in the kitchen, panicking over whether the food was good enough for a count.

'What have you done?' I asked.

'Garlic prawns, followed by steak and kidney pie. I know you like that.'

'Lovely mother. I expect it will be a first for Simon, but he is not a fussy man. Honestly, don't worry about it. He is just pleased to be here.'

'Are you having an affair with him?'

'Since his wife died, he has turned to me. I brought him back from the dead. He was in a coma for five days and I sat by his bedside all that time, just going to the hotel to sleep. He has always loved me, you know. I have loved him from the moment we met, but he said I was too young.'

'And your studies?'

'Oh yes. We study hard. He wants me to succeed. I do too. I have to have a career, and I want to help people in this World. Nothing will stop me from becoming a doctor. You do like him?'

'Oh yes, of course. I think you are a very lucky girl. When I think back..... I am very proud of my children. Your brother, he is such a gentleman now. When I think back, such a little bully, the things he said to you, his language, I don't know where he heard such things. And I did too, at least I thought things. I regretted having you at one time, such shame, the neighbours whispering. But now, you come here, a great lady. I don't even recognise that little boy we packed off to boarding school. I'm glad. I wish we saw more of you Trudi, my little girl.'

'I will ask Simon if you can come to the Château for a holiday mummy. I would love you to see it. And no, he has not bought me, although he is very generous. I really love him, from that first moment we met. Fortunately, he also loves me. Do you know, he took all the fashion staff on the Bateaux Mouches, and presented me with that car outside, for being with him when he was so injured? I think I am the luckiest student in Paris.'

'Lovely darling, as long as he is not using you, or you him.'

'Mummy, you know me by now. And Simon! Well he could have any woman in the World. He has money, a title and is handsome. He is also a very big player in fashion. Any woman would throw themselves at his feet. He has chosen me. It is very flattering. A reassurance of who I am.'

'Yes dear of course. I just needed to know.'

'And you still don't, do you? You will still worry, whatever. If the worst comes to the worst, I will have a career, my own income. That is why I have to study. Be happy for me. Simon has taught me how to be a lady, introduced me to fine wine and food, and people and how to dress. If he finally rejects me, then I have learned so much of value for an independent future.'

'You sound so French dear. I hardly recognise your voice.'

We ate dinner. Simon paid compliments on the steak and kidney, liked the pepper and the gravy. He asked father and mother to come over to the Château. We stayed one more day and moved to Cambridge.

We found Sam happy with her boy friend and her course in Cambridge. Her father looked older but was, he said, well enough. Her mother took me in her arms and held me away examining me. 'What a lady. You have grown up so. Kleine Trudi, liebchen.' She turned to Simon. 'You are very welcome. It is good to meet you at last.'

We stayed two days, walking around the colleges, taking a punt, all six of us, to Grantchester with a picnic and fine wine. I visited school and saw the Hendersons. It all looked just the same, in fact smarter but also smaller than my memory of it. It was of course holiday time, so there were no pupils. We drank tea and kissed as I left.

It was time to go back to the prosthesis maker for an adjustment where the stump rubbed. How I hated that word, stump. They took a new mould, altered the fitting and noted all the details in case they needed to make another.

It was with some relief that we headed for Newhaven and the ferry. I could not wait to return to the Château.

Simon was very tired when we arrived. We had a snack supper, cooked by me, some chicken breasts in a tomato, basil and olive sauce, throwing in some fresh spinach at the last minute and sauté potatoes. I assisted him up to bed, frightened that we would have another accident on that marble staircase. He went to his room and I saw him into bed, saying that I would not be long. I sat with Gérard and Annette for a while, before I too went up. I bathed and dressed in a nice nighty and instead of going to my room, climbed in beside him.

He was out completely, did not even realise I was there. I snuggled gently towards him and was soon asleep too. I woke early. Simon slept on and I did not disturb him. Eventually he began to wake and I cuddled up, slinging one leg over him. I noticed how grey he had become. He looked distinguished, but I thought, ten years older than a year ago.

It was some time before he responded. Then he gripped me tightly around my waist, as if to squash me into him. I felt for him, but he said no, just cuddle me. After a while I left the bed, showered and dressed. I made for the nursery and found that Sophie was wrestling with the three little ones. I fed Sébastien with a bottle, burped him over my shoulder walking around the room. We took them all downstairs and out onto the lawn in the sunshine. We spread two large blankets on the ground and let the twins run riot. Little Sébastien remained in his pram the hood over so that he was not staring at the bright sky. He was soon asleep while the twins romped, throwing themselves on each other and us. We tried to teach them hand-slapping games, but they were still too young to really get it, but it amused them.

Simon appeared walking with two sticks, and one of the staff brought a garden chair for him.

'It is time for your riding lesson,' he said, 'I know you are having fun, but I would really like you to ride.'

'Of course. Now you are here, Sophie will be able to manage, but three little ones is quite a task and it will get worse as Sébastien becomes more active. I think she should have a maid to help. Is there not in the village, a young girl who could do with pocket money?'

'I will think about it Trudi. Thank you. Now go for your lesson.'

I dressed in the full kit, even did my makeup then descended to the stables. I found a Sabine there dressed in jodhpurs and boots. Two horses were saddled ready.

'Enfin,' she said. (At last).

'I did not know that you were waiting. Le Comte has just told me, then I had to get ready, Simone.'

'Sabine. I have been asked to teach you to ride. So we don't waste time, and no complaining. It will be hard work. I know who you are, I have read the papers. With me you get away with nothing because you are Trudi, model, spoiled little girl.'

'You do not know me Sabine. But you are going to find out.' I put on my last glove and went to the Arab mare Sheba. I untied the reins from the fence, talked to her and stroked her nose, breathed into her so that her nostrils flared, then holding reins and saddle, hoisted myself upon her back. Sabine checked the stirrups, making me rise in the saddle, adjusted them both and looked critically at them.

'Bien.' She hoisted herself effortlessly into her saddle on the large seventeen hands gelding.

'Allons-y.' She motioned me to ride beside her. I kicked the mare into action and we set off down the estate road at a walk.

'Back straighter. Grip with your knees, communicate with the horse, she needs to know you are there and in command. Hands lower. Good.'

We came to the horse gallop that ran round a large paddock, white paddock fences and short grass.

'OK, we trot. Bien, non, no bouncing on the horse back, do you want to cripple her? Oui, better. OK we do one circuit at the trot. You go first so I can see you. Don't let her slow to a walk, keep her trotting, heels and hands all the time. Oui, bon.'

It was torture. My legs soon began to feel the strain, my thighs ached and burned. After a circuit, Sabine came alongside. 'Not too bad. Right stop.' She pulled a leading rein from her saddle bag and attached it to Sheba's bridle.

'Now we canter. You stay in the saddle, no bumping about, keep weight on your stirrups and grip with the knees. Feel the rhythm. You watch me as we go. Imitation. Yes.?

OK we go, go on kick her again, not the trot, kick oui, now she understands what you want. They like to canter, it is natural for them and comfortable for you. Good look at me, you go down in the saddle as the horses back rises, you keep your seat.'

'Stop.' We stopped.

'OK. I have seen worse. So, now we can try a gallop. You bring Sheba to a canter and then you use your heels and set her into a gallop. It is the most comfortable. Are you ready?'

'I am ready Sabine.'

'We go. Kick, kick oui, oui kick. Allons-y.' we galloped up a sandy track into the forest, and it was comfortable and thrilling. 'Stop, bring your horse to a stop, slowly so. It was good, oui?'

'Oui Sabine. It was very good.'

'We can't do that all the time, the horse would die. So now we walk. Then we trot. When possible we canter. You have another hour yet. Tired?'

'Yes, tired. But we go on. Sabine you are strict with me.'

'I have to make you a rider. There is not time enough. At the moment you are terrible. That poor horse, with a sack of potatoes sitting on her.'

I looked at her sideways. She was laughing.

'Sabine you are wicked. A horrible person.'

'And you Trudi the model, are a spoilt rich girl. Why don't you cry and have a tantrum?'

'Because you would like me to.'

'Less talk, trot. No remember what I have said, back straight, surely a model can do that. Are you brainless? Hands lower, go with the horses head. Yes better. You have forgotten everything I taught you before. You are not an idiot?'

She kept on at me for the next hour, finding fault all the time until I dismounted in the stable yard.

'Take off the saddle, like I do. Then take her into the stable. Pet her, she has done well. Brush her down, I'll show you. Take off the bridle, yes that strap and that one. Good. OK, give her some hay and chaff and corn, about this much. Look her water bucket is only half full. Tip that out, rinse and fill.

I did as she told me.

'So Trudi le Model. How do you think you did?

'OK. Better than last time. How do you think I did?'

'Well Trudi le model....'

'Enough Sabine. I am Trudi, student médicin, student équitation, étudiant de la vie. I work hard. I like you. You are a good but tough teacher, but show me some respect, for trying.'

She looked at me sideways. 'Good, now we know where we are. Take off your glove, and the other one. Here is my hand, Mademoiselle Trudi. You did very well, for a beginner. Friends.' She kissed me on both cheeks.

'Tomorrow. Ten o'clock. Don't be late.'

She mounted her horse and was off out of the yard gate.

I found Simon in the salon, the children had gone up to have a nap. He was reading, Gérard and Annette had gone to the local market.

'How was it?'

'It was good. Who is Sabine, Simon?'

'She is a cousin, my father's brother's youngest. They have the grande maison de compagne just outside the village. You don't like her?'

'She didn't seem to like me. She was quite rude and I had to put her in her place.'

'She upset you?'

'Aggressive. No problem. We had words. Now we are fine. I like her, but she is fiery.'

'There is some jealousy and I am afraid, they think Simon and his little English, you say, Bimbo? Oui?'

'Yes, that is exactly what she thought. Simon, I don't like that people think of me, of us like that. I would like you to have a party, invite the local people, perhaps when my parents and Élise and Jean Luc are here. And Vanessa and Elie and John; and their friends too, the ones who gave the party when we first met. Perhaps fancy dress. It would be such fun, and I could meet everyone and they would know me.'

'It is short notice, but if you will do the invitations on the computer in my office, I will make a guest list.'

We set to work immediately. That evening I went in the car to deliver all the local ones by hand, first calling at Sabine's where I asked her to assist me in finding the addresses. By nightfall, we had delivered them all. The others were in the post. I had no doubt that most would accept. They would be as curious and prejudiced about the little English as Sabine had been.

When I returned, Simon was in bed reading a novel.

'So here you are. Are you tired?' He asked.

'Yes. The riding and this evening. I must have a bath Simon. My limbs are aching so.'

'And when you come out of the bath? Will you be tired or will you be available? We have not made love for ages.'

'Shall we see? Maybe you will be too tired.'

I bathed, in warm water, and let the cold run in until I could bear the cold no longer. I got out glowing, feeling immediately warm as the relatively warm air wrapped my body.

I walked to the bed nude, a few drops of water clinging to my moisturised skin. I climbed in and swept the covers back. I had to come to terms with his amputation and get over the horror of it. I took it in my hands and bent my head and kissed it. I imagined it was an elbow, so nothing to fear. I replaced it gently and ran my fingers up his leg, up his thigh and stomach, then both hands up his body until they were behind his neck and I kissed him, gently and hard, softly. He was already fully erect, his penis throbbing with each heartbeat, the head deep rose and oozing, the precum glistening. I massaged his chest, and he groaned with arousal and anticipation.

'What do you want Simon?'

'Baise moi, baise moi.'

'I don't know,' I said feigning reluctance. 'Are you really well enough? I don't think I should.'

'You should, really you should. It has been too long.'

I held him by his penis. I ran a sharp fingernail up it. 'I'm not sure,' I said, my left index finger on my slightly parted lips. 'I think I am a little tired from riding. No, not to night Napoleon. Good night.' I pretended to go.

'Come back here, you bitch. Baise moi now.'

I leapt astride him, taking his breath away, grasping him firmly and inserting him into my wet vagina. 'There, is that better? Is this what you want the little English bimbo for?'

'You act like a lady and fuck like a whore,' he said, 'and I love it.'

I rode him gently, not letting him climax, keeping him on simmer, the pain of ecstasy never far from his lips. I pinched his nipples hard so that he bucked with sudden pain, and I rode him fast to a finish. We lay joined, with no covers over us until we drifted off to sleep. I woke in the night and pulled the sheet up.

Chapter 20.

Over breakfast, Simon studied his diary.

'I have to go to the Maison Beauvonne tomorrow and I want you to come too. Tell Sabine no riding, or she will be cross again. You will drive me. In ten days time we have the show, and you will be in it. There are three dresses for you to wear, so tomorrow we do the fitting. Your parents and your friends are here at the time of the show too, so we must take two cars. The big Mercedes is automatic, so I will drive that. There will be enough seats for all. After the show, we have the usual party. It will be good for your parents to see you as a model, we will let your mother behind the scenes, I think she will enjoy and Élise, I want to do something for her. She would not model I think, no but we give a makeover and put her on the floor seating people, yes, I think so.'

'Lovely idea Simon, thank you. Then our party, two days after the show? I need a costume.'

'I thought, if you agree, a ballet dancer, white tutu, ballet shoes, hair piled up in a golden bun and a gold mask on a stick. What do you think?'

'Perfect. It will be fun. And Simon, for my parents and Élise and Jean Luc. How should we dress them?'

'I thought your father as an Eastern potentate, complete with curly slippers, your mother in a crinoline I think, like Gone with the Wind, this film you like so much. Jean Luc, a young Napoleon and Élise as Josephine.'

'And you?'

'I will be General de Gaulle. I have the nose for it. I will order the outfits today. I will ask Robert to come and manage the food, a good buffet.

'Jean Luc's father and mother move into their cottage at the weekend, so they will be on hand to help. Of course Annette and Gérard will not be here, they will be on their cruise in the Caribbean. You know Simon, they said they were going to marry and I was to be a bridesmaid, but they must have changed their minds. Do you know what happened?

'No, but I think Annette may have found Gérard is less than perfect.'

'Is he?'

'Oh yes, he has failings, drink and gambling.

'Oh and I got him more involved in Beauvonne.'

'Yes, never mind. He has done me a favour so giving him steady work is recompense. So what else have we to do for this party?'

'I will have costumes for all the staff too.'

Sabine and I rode. I was getting to love Sheba, I just hoped she did not hate me lumping about on her back. Sabine really put me through my paces again. It was intensive and every little error was picked up and snorted at.

However, at the end she said, 'Very well done. You try hard Trudi. There is hope.'

In the afternoon I played with the children when they awoke from their slumber and helped give them tea. Then it was bath time and I bathed the twins while Sophie attended to Sébastien. When they were tucked up in their cots, I bathed and changed for dinner. In the salon, we were all drinking cocktails when Sophie entered. She looked lovely too, all scrubbed up. She thanked me for my help. 'Sophie, I do it because I love those babies. It is your job, but I love being with them and it is good for you to have more time.'

'I love them already, Trudi. I love this job.' I could see she did. Annette had made a brilliant choice. Sophie was relaxed with them, unflustered, tender yet firm. She did not raise her voice, just changed her tone when she had to bring the twins to order.

I went to bed very tired, with the light still in the sky and I was soon asleep.

Simon and I rose early. He dressed in his grey pin stripe and there was a slight twenties tone to his outfit. He only needed spats to look like Maurice Chevalier, carrying a silver topped ebony cane. He looked very debonair. Today he said, he would walk into Maison Beauvonne, without sticks. He had been practising. I drove him in my lovely Mercedes and we made the salon in two and a half hours. I stopped outside and he stepped into the salon, stick over his arm. I parked the car at the rear.

I entered through the cutting room, shaking hands with people and kissing as I went. It was like being part of the family. I found Simon with the designers, talking through the running order.

I was brought a coffee and sat listening. Mostly it was about finance and customers. The meeting broke up and we all went to the rails to see the dresses I would wear. There was one from the readymade collection, fitted bodice, black and white diagonal stripes across the hips accentuating the figure and a pencil skirt. It was very nice, designed to appeal to the middle market. Very wearable.

The two haute couture dresses were just thrilling. The first was gold, fitted and tightly pleated across the bust, reminiscent of a Grecian goddess, with a train, the other was a bit punky, a wired wide skirt, which would rise and fall with each step, black organza with pearls sewn into the bodice. I had a fitting and a few adjustments were pinned so that it would fit perfectly on the day. It was so exciting to be back. I was shown pictorials of how my hair and makeup would be.

The punk one was tremendous. As long as they didn't cut my hair off, I did not mind.

Simon showed me the outfit Élise would wear, a sleek teadress in white with a diagonal stripe, a dress she could keep afterwards and wear.

We lunched at Willi's again with Thomas, Jacques and the senior dressmakers, Vivienne and Greta. I loved being with these creative and vivacious people. This was where I felt truly secure.

It was time to drive home. I arrived home in time to put the children to bed. Sébastien had his bottle, I spent half an hour burping him. I changed his nappy and put him in his cot. I rocked him to sleep. The twins had a little play, were bathed and dressed and settled down in their cots. Simon came up to the nursery and watched.

I had half an hour to wash and change and go to dinner. It had been another long day. After dinner, I said au revoir to Gérard and Annette. They were departing early for their holiday next morning. I went straight to bed in my own room. I woke at three, and climbed into Simon's bed. I woke at eight, and Simon was still asleep. I tiptoed out and bathed. Then I went to the nursery. Sophie was already at work. I fed Sébastien and changed him. He was very active this morning, kicking and giggling when I tickled him. It was a delight.

Three days later my parents arrived. I took them up to their room. They were just astounded. When they were settled I showed them my room, then the nursery. I took them down for tea with Simon. After tea he showed them the estate, driving his big Mercedes, while I helped Sophie.

The chef had put on a special dinner. Moules marinières, roast leg of lamb with flagelot beans, chocolate coconut pudding and orange sauce. We sat talking after the coffee. Simon was very charming, putting them at ease. He explained what the programme was, including the trip to Paris and the fancy dress party. Next day we took them to the Normandy beaches. We had seafood on the harbour at Courseulles-sur-Mer., Juno Beach, where the Canadians and the Royal Marines came ashore. Grandfather had been amongst them, but had survived the slaughter. Father was both excited and quiet, thoughtful. Mother looked at her guidebook and read us passages. We retuned well before dinner and mother and I went to the nursery. I gave her Sébastien to feed. We put the children to bed and went to dress for dinner.

The following day, Élise and Jean Luc arrived. I outlined the programme and left them to Simon while I went for my riding lesson. Sabine was her usual brutal self. She conceded that I was making good progress. In the afternoon, we three went for a walk and stopped off at Jean Luc's parents' cottage. It was finished and to a high standard. His parents were very jolly, happy with their move from the apartment in Bourg St Maurice. Jean Luc was impressed. His father would start work in two days' time. Simon was such a good man.

My parents were nervous about the fancy dress party, it was not the sort of thing they did, but they could not but be impressed by their outfits. They asked what I was wearing, but I said it was a surprise. I had been practising some ballet moves and had an exercise bar set up on the terrace that afternoon.

General de Gaulle entered my bedroom and watched as I got ready. I made my face carefully, tied my hair back and kept it there in the elasticised golden bun net. I made my face carefully, with high brows, pink eye shadow and lips, with sparkles on my cheeks. I wore half inch long lashes to accentuate my eyes. I struggled into the tights, then the ballet shoes and finally the tutu, which the General zipped up. I took up my mask and made my way down the stairs and out on to the terrace. Many had arrived already, and I spotted Ellie and company at a table, dressed to the nines. The General was talking to them, and they were joined by Napoleon and Josephine.

I started my exercises on the bar, and pirouetted to the steps, keeping my mask on my face. I pirouetted to where my parents were sitting and disclosed my identity. I moved over to Ellie and the others and brought my parents over to sit with them. Sabine recognised me. She was dressed in a harem outfit and talking to a young man who looked like Robin Hood. Most of the rest I did not know. The tables were soon full of people and as night drew on, candles were lit on the tables and one of the groups started to play Mozart. Later a pop group struck up. General de Gaulle and I danced slowly and others joined in. By the time it was properly dark, the floor was full of dancers. The buffet opened and people ate.

Simon surprised me by tapping his glass with a spoon until there was silence. 'Oh God,' I thought, 'please don't let this be embarrassing.'

'Mesdames et messieurs, mes chers amis. As you see, I am back not quite in one piece,' he tapped his artificial leg with a stick, 'but here I am. I have to thank my dear Trudi for that, because she sat by my bed for many days, talking to me while I was in a coma. I am very grateful for her devotion. I also thank my friend Vanessa for looking after Trudi in that period. Trudi also has two very good friends, fellow student médicins, who share her apartment in Paris, who have helped her and continue to do so, especially while she was not at university but sitting in CCU. So I am indebted to them also.

'I thank all my friends and relations for coming today. This is an opportunity to meet Trudi, my protégé. Some will have read about her in the press. Do not believe all you read. She is not a dumb blonde, a bimbo. She is a clever student, studying médicin in a foreign language. That is difficult. But also, she is loyal, has good judgment and above all, courage. I present to you, Trudi.'

He raised my arm, and made me rise, the tutu escaping from its imprisonment below the table, popping up like a jack in a box. I stepped to the side, pirouetted and curtsied.

I felt compelled to show that I had something to say too.

'Mes amis. I have much to be thankful for, but especially to my parents who supported me and although worried, allowed me at eighteen to live in the wicked city of Paris.' (There was much laughter.) 'Next I wish to thank Élise and Jean Luc, my dear friends who have helped me so much. Thank you to Ellie and Vanessa, for becoming my friends when I really needed them and for introducing me indirectly to my benefactor, Monsieur le Comte de Beauvonne, Simon. I thank Sabine, my ferocious riding instructor. She has not used her whip on me yet, but I am constantly aware she has it in her hand. Merci Sabine.' They all laughed. 'And Sophie, nanny to Simon's babies, for allowing me to play with and tend them. She has taught me much. Have I forgotten anyone? Oh oui, Simon. Thank you for showing me a new life, for your indulgence and help. You also have courage.

People danced and talked, a few got a little drunk, then the company started to drift away, cars started and finally we went to bed.

Next day I was down at the stables on time. Sabine was waiting, even so. We set off immediately, this time just in the school. Round and round I went, while the young martinet yelled at me. Posture, knees, hands, feet. Walking, trotting, cantering. I hated it, restricted by the ring of fences and it was such hard work. As a reward we went for a short hack through the forest, having a little gallop up a sandy lane. Sheba loved it, her head up and snorting her enjoyment.

'Nice speech Trudi,' she said, when we were unsaddling. 'Thank you. However, I will not let up. You have a lot of catching up to do, but I think perhaps we are going in the right direction. You did well today. So tomorrow, it is Trudi le model, oui? OK. I hope all goes well.'

'Me too. I love it, but if I slip on a heel or the dress catches, disaster.'

'Trudi, be careful. Oui? Sometimes all is not as it seems. I see you in two days. On Friday. We do a lot of work on control of the horse. Bon chance Trudi. Those heels, they are dangerous.'

Chapter 21.

We set out for Paris, my parents with me and Élise and Jean Luc with Simon. In the salon all was organised chaos, people rushing about, girls in various stages of dress, hair stylists at work and makeup artists too.

Simon looked after Élise, explaining the duties of an usher at such an event. He gave her the frock and sent her into makeup and hair, because she would be on show to the public first. Jean Luc just looked goggle eyed until he was shushed out into the auditorium to sit with my parents. I had three different looks. Firstly as a career girl, in heavy rimmed spectacles in the ready made, then with funky lurid makeup for the punk dress, and lastly looking like a goddess in gold.

At last the audience were all assembled. The models were lined up ready to go. There would be two three or four of us in the ready made gear on the catwalk at a time, forming tableaus, round the copier machine which came out of the floor. It all needed split second timing to carry it off, and no hurrying. I did my strut, we posed, the audience applauded and we dispersed. Back in the changing room the dress was peeled from me. Sitting in bra and knickers my punk makeup and hair was completed, then on with the dress and platform shoes. I looked in the mirror, My hair was piled up on one side of my head, kept there by a transparent sort of trellis. My cheeks were purple and magenta, my eyes black, lips large magenta and pouting. This time I was alone on the catwalk. I reached the end, turned left, turned right, thrust a hip out and looked haughty. I turned and made it back safely. The house erupted in applause.

Another change. All makeup off and a different face and hairdo, then on with the heavy gold dress. The bodice seemed to weigh a tonne, and I thought it would slip off, but the clever boning and skin tight fit on my hips, kept me respectable. At last we all entered the catwalk, and formed tableaus all the way down, a hand on a shoulder, rocking back from the waist as though laughing, shaking hands or turning to speak to someone. As the applause reached a crescendo, Simon and the designers walked on. It was over. I cleaned my face and did my street make up, and we went to the apartment to rest and freshen up before the after show party.

Simon returned at five with the first reviews of the show. It was a tremendous success, especially the new ready-made designs that the large stores were fighting to get. I received another new dress from Simon, a pure white prom dress with black silk around the bust line and waist and a tulip skirt. It was just gorgeous. I wore my diamond choker, but then thought it too much. In the end I just wore the Rolex and some large drop earings in yellow and white gold and diamonds. A black clutch and white heels completed the outfit.

Simon inspected me minutely. 'Yes, every inch a lady, looking so pure, yet I know you are so sexy in private. You are so desirable, every man there tonight will want to conquer you, yet you belong to this old cripple.'

'Not so old, and not so much a cripple. You are walking quite well now. That slight limp is intriguing mon plus cher.'

I went into Simon's salon to see mother and make sure she felt comfortable, and she burst into tears when she saw me. 'I don't know where my little boy went to,' she said, 'it is as though he died and you have taken his place, a completely different person.'

'Come,' I said, 'see my apartment.' Father followed and we went through the separating door. Mother was charmed with it. I made tea and they settled down. Simon reappeared dressed for the evening, then Jean Luc and finally Elise in the emerald dress I had given her. We took taxis to Olympia. A black pianist played old musical hits while we ate. I recognised 'Anything Goes,' 'Every Time We Say Goodbye,' and 'Night and Day'. When the meal was finished, Simon made one short speech, thanking everyone for holding Beauvonne together and making it a great success.

The pianist was joined by the rest of the band and they played swing and traditional jazz. The floor filled, I danced with so many, and especially my father that felt like a stamp of approval. Simon claimed me for the last dance, managing to make it round the floor with me, before we bade everyone good night and went home.

Three days later, my parents went home. I was quite relieved not to have the responsibility. Élise and Jean Luc went to her home. I got down to Sabine's intensive horse riding course. I felt more confident each time and Sheba now seemed to look for me when I entered the yard.

After two weeks I picked my friends up and we reported to our various hospitals for our unpaid nursing duties. August in Paris, and it was hot and empty, well of those who could afford to leave for the seaside or countryside. The month went quickly. I loved being busy, talking to the patients and being helpful.

I went back to the Château for two weeks. Simon was not always there, off globe trotting again, selling his creations. I spent time with Sabine and we would sometimes ride all day, stopping at a café in a village for lunch and a drink. I would help Sophie too. Simon had not got her any help, I suppose seeing that I was happy to be a surrogate mother. These were wonderfully happy weeks. All too soon, it was September and we returned to Paris for another year of toil. Two years done. This year would be the last of DCEM

1, more lectures and book learning before going on to practical learning on the wards and clinics.

La Pitié Salpêtrière was like an old friend. We knew our way around, and Paris was a second home to the Château where I was truly happy. The autumn was golden until the end of October, the leaves hung on the plain trees for dear life until the weather changed overnight. Cold slanting rain poured in from the East. The leaves left the trees as the umbrellas blossomed. Lights were reflected off wet pavements even in daytime. Then the rain stopped and the cold grew even more intense. Simon appeared regularly, sleeping with me for a night then zooming off again. One or two weekends I managed to go to the Château, taking Jean Luc to see his parents and dropping Élise at her farm. Sabine taught me riding.

In spite of our bad beginning, Sabine and I were now good friends.

'So Sabine, you know about me. Tell me about yourself.'

'Oh that will be quickly done Trudi. I am not an exotic creature like you. My father is cousin to Simon. Our farm is under a thousand hectares, so I am a real country girl. I went to University and I have a degree in agriculture, a very good degree. I have a brother Laurent who works with father on the farm.'

'So why don't you work on your farm?'

'Because I do not agree with how father runs the business. He disapproves of girls running farms and with University farm degrees. He is so old fashioned and we have always rowed. I want to change it all, but he farms as his father did except he has machinery. Laurent goes along with what father says, mostly, knowing that one day the farm will be his and I will get money for my share. But I want to farm. Meanwhile, here I am, having fun with my pretty little pupil. Now, it is your turn. Oh yes I have read OK and other things, mother cuts everything out about you and puts them in a book. But what I cannot understand is how you got to where you are now. Why did a boy baby want to be a girl? I am happy as a girl, but for practicable purposes, I would rather have been a boy. Laurent has more freedom, more fun. So what made you want to be a girl?'

'I was just born, hating being what I was, even before I knew what a girl was. Just as a chick in a bird's nest knows that if it drops out and flaps its wings, it will fly, I knew I did not want to be a boy and also I wanted long hair, frocks, nice skin, gentleness. As I realised the difference, the pain grew stronger. At eight I asked a girlfriend to show me her privates and I instinctively wanted to be the same. That was when things came to a head. The neighbour, mother of the girl and my mother, thought to teach me a lesson by dressing me as a girl. I felt shamed but deep down I knew they were giving me exactly what I wanted. Mother then read some books and understood a bit more, so I became a girl at home and a boy at school, until I was sixteen, then I dressed as a girl all the time and was taking hormones. So here I am.'

'Were you bullied?'

'Oui, but I found by staying aloof, cutting people with my tongue and not showing fear, bullies would almost always show me respect.'

'Like you treated me, when I thought to bully you.'

'Yes Sabine. Why did you?'

'Perhaps I was a bit jealous. Trudi, le modèle, so beautiful and clever and the pet of Simon de Beauvonne. What I had read in the papers and suddenly you were thrust into my care and I was ordered to make you a horsewoman. But I offered my hand, did I not?'

'Yes Sabine and I am glad to have you as my friend. But you, you cannot be content to be a groom all your life. Have you a boyfriend?'

'Only geldings. Horses are a substitute. Something will turn up. I have applied to be a farm manager, been shortlisted but they always want someone experienced.'

'Sabine, I hope you find something, but not before you have made me a rider. And promise we will always be friends.'

'Of course.'

'No really. Like the Gypsies.' I spat on my hand and offered it to her. She smiled, did the same and we shook hands. I kissed her on the lips. Then I felt self-conscious and blushed.

She laughed. 'You are so girlie, Trudi le modèle. Be careful or I may really like you. But be careful anyway. It is time we rode back.'

A week later Simon rode for the first time since the accident. He was ecstatic at my progress and praised Sabine for her efforts. I swelled with pride.

Simon was again busy. I implored him to find someone to help with sales, but he would not. He seemed to be permanently living out of a suitcase. 'Anyway,' he said, 'I enjoy it.'

Christmas this year was much more relaxed, without the overbearing Catherine and the aggressive sulkiness of Françoise. The children were a wonderful asset, the twins now 23 months and Sébastien 10 months were a handful. At last Simon had succumbed to my nagging and a girl came from the village to help Sophie, but I was still a constant visitor to the nursery.

Christmas Eve this year saw us with different guests. Annette and Gérard were in Paris but going to join us at the chalet. Sabine and her mother and father and Laurent joined us to replace them. It was an excellent evening. I had forbidden Simon from giving me another dress and I came down in my red silk. Simon was exceedingly merry, joking and laughing. His business was doing very well and he was thinking of buying a factory in the Auvergne where prices and wages were low, to mass-produce some lines. The meal went on forever, and as delicious as the food and wine was, I ate sparingly. Sabine watched me. I caught her and she smiled.

Afterwards in the salon, some played cards while Sabine and I talked.

'What do you think of the Beauvonne estate Sabine?'

She laughed. 'It is a joke. So much rubbish lying about, land not producing anything, the forest needs thinning and replanting. The seasons are not followed correctly, ploughing and sowing so late sometimes and the hedges not cut, the roads potholed. It is terrible.'

'Oh, I have not seen all that. I just thought that was how it should be. I think Simon is preoccupied with fashion. You have opened my eyes Sabine.'

We were interrupted by laughter as Simon told Sabine's father a tale.

Next day we had the present giving. I had told Simon that I did not want the extravagance of last year, but I thought he would disregard my request.

I had bought toys for the children, dipped into my rather flush bank account and bought them electric motorbikes, mini BMWs with stabilizers. They were a bit young for them as yet but by the next Christmas, I was sure they would be whizzing around. It cannot be too soon to ride something. For little Sébastien I had bought a load of plastic bricks.

For Simon, I had the best fountain pen I could afford, a gold Mont Blanc. Sophie I gave a set of silk underwear. Simon gave me a new ski suit, saying that he realised I had everything and I was quite right to not be greedy. I was disappointed, but smiled my way out of it. In the afternoon I walked down to Sabine's. I had bought her new riding boots and a silver handled whip. I also gave her silk undies. She gave me a new phone as she said, the old one she had seen me with was so last century. We walked out behind her hay barn with a shot gun. She put a toe on a foot switch and two clay pigeons appeared, both of which she hit. She attempted to teach me to shoot, making sure the butt was actually on my shoulder, pulled in tight. She launched a clay and I fired. I missed. I must have missed the next ten. Then I hit one. It was terrific luck. Five more misses while she laughed at me, then I hit another and the next. She launched two and I missed both. I gave up, my shoulder now feeling bruised.

Sabine walked me back to the Château, but stopped at the wrought iron gates. 'Trudi, thank you for bringing my presents. You are very generous. When shall I come to Paris?'

'When you like. Just ring me on my new phone. Really, we can find room for you anytime. I would love you to come.'

'I will. But Trudi, take care. You must not be dazzled by all this.' She waived at the estate and the Château, 'nor your fine clothes and Mercedes.'

'What do you mean?'

'Just remain true to yourself. Remember you are the most important person in your world.'

I remembered the advice someone else had given me. The first person you love is yourself.

'I know, I am careful to make sure I have another world to go to, my career as a médecin. But I can't help but love Simon and his world, the children, my horse, the Château and fashion. I'll see you soon I hope.'

She kissed me, on both cheeks and then my lips, turned on her heel and walked away. I went up the drive. I looked back, and so did she. She waived then broke into a run and disappeared around the bend.

With Sophie, I put the children to bed. I went into my bedroom and found six wrapped boxes on my bed. I opened the first, a Hermes handbag. The second was la Perla underwear. The next contained a Bognor jeans leather jacket, so soft it felt like heavy silk. The next contained leather jeans also soft and supple. The next was leather boots, Bally Renovas. The last was a key and a note which just said, in the stable. I went down and there on the saddle horse was the most gorgeous saddle, beautiful embossed leather side panels, a deep seat and soft rolls to protect Sheba and deep knee rolls to protect my legs. I found Simon in the salon. I knelt and kissed his hand. He sat me on his knee and kissed me.

'As though I would give you nothing. Silly girl,' he said. I remembered sitting on Father's knee, when I had first been put into a skirt. It seemed another life. It was another life.

Chapter 21.

Next morning we left early for the Alps. Simon said he did not want to drive so I drove my beautiful Mercedes. We stopped as usual for lunch and it was only then that I realised I would have to negotiate the road up to Courchevel. We passed through Moutier and turned right up the valley which separates the Courchevel 3 Valleys area from the La Plagne complex. We were soon negotiating the

Z bends and I found it was not nearly as daunting as I had thought from the passenger seat. I noticed Simon squirming once or twice and squeezed his knee. Once the first section was negotiated, the rest of the road up was not so frightening and we were soon in the garage and unloading our luggage. Robert as usual was all efficiency, but on his own this time as his wife was expecting a baby. It was intensely cold.

Simon and I took the bubble to Jardin Alpin. It was freezing without ski clothing. At the chalet we found Annette and Gérard and glorious warmth. We sat down to the usual tea and cake and caught up. Annette admired my leather jacket and my lovely warm boots, which of course with four inch heels, had been totally inappropriate for negotiating the path to the chalet. 'Oh well,' she said, 'You are only young once.'

They discussed the next day's skiing. Pierre, Jean Luc's father was taking them off piste, too much for me, so I would go with Liz. We all went down to the ski room to check that our gear was all in order and found Pierre there waxing all the skis with a hot iron and melting wax. I like the smell. I found I had new skis, which he said, would be better for my ability.

Pierre made me sit and put my boots on with a thin ski sock. He did each buckle up and adjusted the tensions. At his command I stood, bent my knees forward, stamped my feet and bent and sat again. He checked them all again. 'Not too tight eh? If it is too tight it will restrict the blood and you get cold feet, then your legs get tired. You wear all day, so they need to be comfortable. These boot fitters, think you are all downhill racers. Racers need an exact fit. They wear their boots for 10 minutes, not like you. You will be OK. I look forward to seeing you ski.'

'Merci Pierre. Vous êtes trés gentil.'

I went up to our suite. It was like coming home. This was after all, the birthplace of the posy. Simon lay asleep on the bed. He had not recovered from his accident and had then thrown himself into his work and ignored my pleas to slow down. I busied myself, quietly unpacking. I worried about him. He had lost the joie de vivre he possessed eighteen months ago. Even though the death of Catherine and departure of Françoise had been a relief, he had not recovered his easy-going nature.

I lay in the bath with salts and bath oil, lazily sponging myself. I came out and dried. I thoroughly moisturised against the dry mountain air that would suck moisture out of my skin. I sat in my new undies and made my face, then as we usually did, dressed for this first meal of the holiday. I wore the silver dress I had worn in the summer on the Bateaux Mouches.

I turned to find Simon watching me. He patted the bed for me to sit by him.

He sniffed at my neck, then again.

'What are you doing?' I asked.

'Drinking you in. Consuming you. It is strange, so strange. When we first met, it was a matter of cathartic release after the death of my brother, and I have to say, sympathy. Then I was intrigued by the androgyny, knowing who you were but your appearance belying all that. Now...........I just find you bewitching, I cannot understand how you go through your life conquering all. You don't complain, you do not beg. When there is a crisis, you do not panic. I put you on the catwalk, it is a triumph, then again a disaster. You are cornered by journalists in Venice, but you do not lose your head, you face it head on and conquer them. You beautiful sexy woman, you play with my children and nurse them. I make you ride and it is hard work. Even today, I refuse to drive, so you drive 850 kilometres, nine hours and a mountain road. It is impossible. That is why when I see you, I cannot believe what I see. That is why I love you so. Always believe that, even when I am bad tempered.'

'I have not seen you bad tempered. As far as my life is concerned, mon cher, I do what I have to do or because I want to. How else to live this life? I am just Trudi. I am blessed with pleasant looks and a brain and the stamina to work hard. Much of that comes from being happy, certain of who I am, and much of that has come from you too. When we met, I was a gauche little girlie boy in fancy dress. You have made me a lady.'

'Non ma petite. You were always a lady, just trying to escape your ugly chrysalis. I must get washed and dressed. We have company.'

I went down before him, reading an article on the British Royal Family in OK magazine. They all seemed so foreign, and I realised that I was becoming French. I was still proud of my English heritage, but I also enjoyed my French life. All my most enjoyable moments had been here in La Belle France. Annette and Gérard entered, then Simon. There was a ring of the doorbell and Vanessa and Ellie appeared. I was overwhelmed. I embraced them as if they were my own, and tears filled my eyes. Simon's speech had aroused so many old memories, this reunion with such dear and intimate friends, had brought emotional overload.

Champagne corks popped and I recovered composure. Ellie sat by me and held my hand. Simon saw but smiled as only someone can who has absolute trust. She engaged me with stories of her work. Afghanistan, then the Middle East and back to Pakistan, even a spell in Iran until warned to leave. She told me of an affair with an Afghan girl, and assisting her to the UK as a refugee. She was she said, loudly, in love with the girl. 'She hasn't your je ne sais pas quoi , but she is beautiful, vulnerable and clever. I think I am in love.'

Everyone laughed. I squeezed her hand. 'I am so glad for you Ellie. Now perhaps, you will stop pestering me.'

'Oh I still love you too. So Simon, you be good to her, or she may turn to me.'

'I don't think so Ellie. Simon is the love of my life.'

Annette kissed my cheek. 'Enough. So what is the plan for tomorrow?' Simon told them. Vanessa opted to come with Liz and I.

Jean Luc's mother entered with a tureen. Messieurs et Mesdames, le diner.'

We began with lobster bisque. The fish was sole bonne femme and the main rosemary lamb, saute potatoes and red cabbage.

I was tired after the drive and left before the sweet. I never heard Simon. I woke next morning refreshed. It was seven thirty and the dawn had begun. Everything outside looked grey white, but the sky was uninterrupted blue. It promised to be a lovely day.

I dressed and roused Simon. He was surprised to see me fully dressed. 'The snow is waiting for us Simon. It is a big day for you. With your new leg. I hope you will be all right mon cher. Promise me you will be careful and not do too much?'

'You promise me, we will make love tonight. I want you now.'

'Good things are worth waiting for. If your leg gets tired, just think posy and how much I love you.'

After breakfast the experienced skiers soon departed, but it was arranged that we would all eat lunch just above 1650. I wanted to know that Simon was managing.

The morning went quickly. Vanessa skied well but slowly, while I wanted to whizz down hill at the expense of style, Liz screaming at me and skiing alongside making me copy her attitude. Then she insisted on skiing ahead. 'It's copycat time, you have to do everything I do, exactly. So you try your best and I will be watching.'

By lunchtime I had improved. Having Liz in front to model myself on helped enormously. We covered a lot of ground, even came down from Saulire and I wasn't terrified. We arrived to find their party already at the table. I sat next to Simon.

'How was it. How did you get on.' I asked.

'OK. I can ski on one ski, so having one and a half is a bonus. I was fine, you should not worry.'

I was so relieved. After lunch we all skied together. Simon was pleased at my progress. We did some red runs, quite slowly me while the others raced ahead and waited at the bottom.. As the light faded we made for home. I was ready for tea, crusty pain de compagne baguette and butter and marmite. Lemon drizzle cake and tea. Oh so lovely. My feet too, in soft lamb skin slippers relaxed after wearing boots all day.

I had stripped off to slip into the bath when Simon came into the room.

'Look at my leg for me please.'

I looked and there was a raw patch where it had blistered and burst.

'Oh Simon, that must be painful. What can we do.'

'Put a plaster on it.'

'No, I don't think so. I would keep it dry, hope that it dries overnight and tomorrow we will put a large blister plaster on it. If that does not work we will go to the medical centre.'

'Thank you doctor. You will have to help me in the bath then.'

I helped him into the bath, keeping his stump over the side out of the water and steam. I searched my medicines for anything for it. I tried iodine, the new sort without the burning pain. Mother always told me when I came home with grazed knees that the stinging iodine was a sign that it was doing good. Iodine has come back into fashion, now it does not hurt. It is not only a strong antiseptic, it has drying qualities, reacting with the serum which oozes from a blister or graze.

I got into the bath too and washed him thoroughly. Simon washed my posy, it was very arousing and I could not get us out of the bath soon enough. I dried him down and helped him to the bed. As he sat I grabbed his penis and sucked him. His hands embedded themselves in my hair and gripped me so tightly I could hardly move. He came remarkably quickly. I lay on the bed and he started to work on me. I tried to stay absolutely still, as though his magic was not working but as he moved up my legs to my thigh I put my nails into his back. He teased. He stopped. He looked into my face and laughed. He began again, circling around my posy, tracing the flowers and the frame, stroking down my clit, so that my buttocks clenched. He sucked each breast in turn making me gasp, opening me, feeling my wetness, savouring it with his tongue. He launched himself upon me, entering, penetrating, until I was completely filled by him

He pumped me until I wanted to scream, and I came first bucking into him to make him stop, but he would not until he came as well. We lay together for an hour.

We washed again and dressed for dinner, casually as Liz was expected as well as Ellie and Vanessa.

It was a merry party, Gérard performing his party tricks and Ellie was at her riotous best. Vanessa was dignified as usual, shushing her daughter's exuberances ineffectively. Liz looked really feminine, in a beautiful chiffon blouse and jeans. Simon sat holding my hand as much as possible. He had drunk a lot by the time the sweet was produced.

Vanessa asked him how he was doing with his new leg.

'This is my new leg,' he said, raising my hand aloft. 'I depend on her for my wellbeing and my happiness. I will marry her if she will have me? Will you do me the greatest honour and become la Comtesse de Beauvonne?' He produced as if by magic a ring box, not velvet covered, but mother of pearl. He opened it. There was a large diamond, then snaking down each side of the ring, alternate sapphires and diamonds. The party looked surprised, then clapped, suddenly stopping, waiting for my reaction.

I kissed him, blushing, surprised and confused. I said nothing for a moment and a hush descended.

'You know Simon that you are the light of my life. I am willing to be engaged to you if that is what you want. But I also want a long engagement, at least eighteen months. I say this because it is only seven months since Catherine had her accident, and also I feel I am still too young and have so much to learn. If you can accept these terms, then I am not going to disappoint you, but there is no announcement, no public knowledge. This stays between us here.'

'If that is all you want, then it is easy for me to agree.'

He slipped the ring on my finger, and as he did so all my emotions, so controlled until now, welled to the surface. My face crumpled, and tears welled, I hid my face and left the table. I went to my room and sat on the bed. Vanessa knocked and entered.

'That is a really strange reaction,' she said. 'What troubles you?'

'I..........,' and I blubbed out loud and uncontrolled.

'I am so happy. Vanessa you know everything about me. For him to love me so. I am too lucky.'

'You deserve him. I am so proud to have, well in my way, put you on this road. When I think how I used you to get Tom off our backs, and getting those pressies, I am so ashamed, yet you bear no grudges, for anyone nor for your birth into a wrong body. No there is no doubt, he is the winner. You honour him. Now come back to the table, there is champagne and toasts.'

We returned. Toasts were made to us and we toasted back to our very good friends. I loved the ring, could not stop looking at it. It was just wonderful.

We went to bed at around one. In seven hours we would rise to get on the slopes by ten.

Chapter 22.

We skied over the next five days, Jean Luc and Élise joining us. I glowed. I showed Élise my ring and for the first time, saw her quite emotional. Jean Luc just kissed me and said congrats. Boys.

I kept looking at the ring, could not believe that this had happened. Simon was very gentle, no more surprises and slightly off demands. He treated me with great consideration and tenderness.

It was finally time to depart. Annette and Gérard would drive Simon back to Normandy and I would drive to Paris with my friends. Ellie and Vanessa were returning to England. The chalet would be empty.

The drive to Paris was uneventful and we were soon back in the apartment and getting ready for University again. The first weeks of January were intensely cold, then the weather turned mild. The last weekend I decided to go to the Château. I phoned Sabine and asked if she would give me riding lessons and happily she was available. Simon would be away, in Japan and then China.

I looked forward to seeing Sophie and playing with the babies as well as riding and just being there, at the Château in the lovely French countryside. I asked Sabine if she would like to come to Paris when I returned, She decided she would.

I left at eight o'clock Friday night after we three had gone over the week's work, so my conscience was clear. I gave my comrades a chance to come, but they refused, I think looking forward to having the apartment to themselves.

I was let in by the housekeeper and made my way to my room. It was strange being there alone. I went straight to bed, locking my bedroom door against what, I had no idea.

I woke quite early and went up to the nursery. Sophie was her usual bright self. We bathed the children and gave them breakfast in the nursery. I left them and went to get dressed for my riding lesson. Sabine was ready for me, but made me tack up Sheba. It wasn't as difficult as I thought.

We set off and I was relieved to find that we were not going to the school, to go round and round at the trot. We made for the forest and cantered through the wide drive, then as we came to the rising ground, Sabine shouted, 'Come on, race you to the top.' I kicked Sheba into a gallop and hung on for dear life as she accelerated into that lovely smooth movement of a horse in gallop. The cool air made my eyes water and when we stopped breathless and giggling at the end, I pulled my gloves, found a hankie and dabbed my eyes.

Sabine was quick to see my engagement ring. She pulled my hand over and examined it.

'Very nice. I presume it is Simon? I thought it would happen. Congratulations Trudi. He does not deserve you.'

'Why do you say that? You don't like him do you?'

'I like him, I just don't trust him. I tried to warn you, but I couldn't find the right words.'

'Warn me about what?'

'No not now. Now we ride, then we talk. Trotting!'

We trotted,, we cantered, we walked. She shouted orders and criticisms just as normal although her words were burning in my brain. At last we were back in the stable yard, grooming Sheba and bedding her down, changing water, filling her hay net and filling her feed bowl with oats and chaff.

'Come,' she said, 'climb to the top of the hay barn with me.' We climbed the bales to the top.

'Please, do not say anything to anybody. What I say is for you, then it is up to you what you do, but I like you and have to tell you as a friend what I know. Do not interrupt me, this is very difficult. I also feel disloyal to Simon, and I do not want to. I am caught in the middle. You make me a solemn promise, you do not repeat my words or tell anyone what I say.'

'I promise.'

'The day Catherine died, the day Simon had the accident, he was here. I was in the forest with my gun, shooting game. I saw Françoise go with the children, then saw Simon walk back to the Château. He went inside. I sat on a log just inside the narrow drive and had a cigarette. I don't often smoke, but now and again, never at home, they don't approve. I was just finishing the cigarette, when Simon left the Château and ran to the drive which leads to the southern end of the estate he carried a box. I was intrigued so I too ran through the woods and saw him get into a car. He took off at high speed.

'I went home. Later I heard that Catherine had fallen down the stairs and was dead. I said nothing. She was a bitch that one, une salope. I have told no one until now and I will not tell anyone else. I hated her. She wanted me banned from the estate, why I don't know.'

'Are you positive Sabine, it was that day? Perhaps you are mistaken. It might have been another day and his car had broken down.'

'It was that day. How could I make a mistake, with the police over everywhere, asking questions. And it was that day that all the staff had the day off too, 9th May, the day after Victory in Europe day, which they had worked because Catherine had held a party. The domestic staff would come back in the evening. It was said, that there had been an argument on the party day. Catherine had all her friends there. She and Simon had been arguing all week, but they said nothing to the police because Simon is the Comte and a good one, treats staff well, but they all knew things were not good. None of them went to the funeral.

'I do not know Trudi what happened. I only know what I saw.'

'But I phoned him on his mobile. He was in the car en route to Courchevel, just for a rest he said. The call was traced and at the time Catherine died, he was a hundred miles away.'

'I know what I know. I have told you for your own safety. I understand that you love him and I think he must love you too. But if that ring means you marry him, then you needed to know.'

'And you are not going to tell anyone else this Sabine?'

'No I have kept this secret and told no one. What will you do?'

'I don't know Sabine. I have to think about it. Thank you for telling me. I know you only want to protect me, but I wish I didn't know.'

I left her and went in. I changed and went to see Sophie. The twins were gambolling around. Sébastien was asleep. I had become really attached, loved being with them.

I took my problem to bed early, and lay there thinking about it. I had phoned Simon the afternoon Catherine died and he had answered and the phone company had identified the mobile as being over 100 miles away. I had thought his voice strange, it had sounded like Gérard. Could it have been? And was Simon driving so fast to make up time that he did not make the bend and went into the ravine? Was I meant to think of the phone as an alibi? I remember, the idea came from Jean Luc but after he had been in to see Simon.

I felt sick. I looked at the engagement ring, thought about taking it off, then left it. Until I spoke to Simon, I could make no decision. It was going to be very difficult.

I had a terrible night. I woke early, showered and dressed. At first I thought of driving back to Paris and trying to find Annette and Gérard. I changed my mind, because that would not be fair either. No this was between Simon and me. Only we could sort out the difficulty between us. He might have an explanation. I loved him and had to trust him.

I met Sabine to ride. She took me to the school and put me through my paces at a distance. As a reward, we then cantered and galloped through the forest. We slowed to a walk. I could smell the scent of the pines and the dead bracken. A dear of some sort sprang across the path some fifty metres ahead. Other than that the wood was silent except for the beat of hooves on the pine needle strewn forest floor and for me the beating of my heart.

'So Trudi. You are very silent. I am sorry. I should not have told you.'

'No. I don't know whether you should or you should not have. I only know that I love Simon and he loves me. If he was responsible for Catherine's death, then I must find out how and why. It is a terrible dilemma. Sabine, be assured, it will make no difference to us, you and I. You must still come to Paris, if you want to and you are my friend, my dear friend. But I have to speak to Simon.'

'I want to come to Paris, but I think this is the wrong time. If Simon comes and finds me there, then he will blame me and we have more family feuding. I want you and I to end the feud, not pour petrol on it. Another time Trudi, and I hope there is an explanation.'

'Rest assured, I shall not disclose what you have told me. He has always pleaded that after the accident, memory of that day was lost to him.'

'Then I will come.' She said.

I spent the afternoon with the children. I could not give them up, nor the Château and above all Simon.

It was three weeks before Simon would have time to come to me, and then it was only going to be overnight. He seemed to be forever in the Far East and the United States, the readymade lines having really taken off. We spoke on the phone then he bought an iPad and we could talk to each other sort of face to face and he could show me where he was with the camera. It was a brilliant way of communicating.

At last the day came and he would be with me in the evening. I went to Uni as usual. We did our work, spending lunch time with a snack and our books, so that we had more free time in the evening. I was home by five and bathed immediately. I dressed with great care in a dress that Marco had given me nearly three years ago. The evening was fine, warm for the end of February, I checked in the mirror. The deep blue prom with pencil skirt four inches above the knee looked classy and under stated. I still wore his ring and I added the diamond cuff and the Rolex. I sat waiting. Seven o'clock came and went. I rang Maison Beauvonne and a cleaner answered. There was no one there. At seven-thirty I was going out of my mind, wondering where he was and whether something had happened. I was about to phone Annette when the phone rang.

A strange voice enquired for me. I replied, yes it was Trudi Nash speaking.

'This is the Pitié Salpêtrière.'

'Oui, I am a student there.'

'Non Mademoiselle, it is not that. We have a patient here, asking for you, Simon de Beauvonne?'

'What has happened.'

'He has had un crise cardiaque. He is not conscious now but he was asking for you. I think you should come. Immediatment mademoiselle.'

I yelled Élise, quickly told her what had happened while I waited for a taxi. She dropped everything and came with me. In fifteen minutes we were running along the corridor to the cardiac department, my heels ringing out each step like a death knell. I stopped at the nursing station and asked for de Beauvonne.

'Oui, attendre ici.'

We sat on some plastic chairs opposite the station. I wanted to howl, but I was numb with shock. After half an hour, I asked again.

'You were too late....'

'He's dead?'

'No mademoiselle. You were too late to see him before surgery. He is now in the operating theatre. As soon as he comes out the surgeon will come and speak to you. I think he will be fine. He has the top man, Professeur Rousse.'

We waited a long time. The clock hands seemed to take an age. Nine o'clock came and went, ten. It was nearly eleven when Rousse appeared still gowned up, mask pulled down. Flecks of Simon's blood on the gown sleeve.

'Come mademoiselle. It took a long time but we were in time and successful. He will live, though he must take care and not work so hard. I recommend he go to his Château and stay there for at least two months. He works too hard I believe. When he was admitted I remembered and sent for you. You can sit with him and wait for him to wake up if you wish.'

He took us to CCU. It was like a recurring nightmare. I asked Élise to go home, but she would not. I sat in CCU, waiting for him to come to. At around one he became conscious. He managed a smile and I kissed him and stroked his greying hair. His colour was better than when I had last seen him.

He drifted off again. I spoke to the nurse. She said he was doing very well and I could come back in the morning. I collected Élise and we rang for a taxi. It was after two when we climbed into bed.

In the morning I asked Jean Luc and Élise to cover for me. I sat in the cardiac department. They moved him into a private room and he was awake and talkative.

'You are sitting by my bed again. We can't keep doing this, you know.'

'And you can't keep rushing round the world and wearing yourself out. The children need you there and I need you too. Simon, this has to end or I will never have the chance to be a widow, for you will be dead before we are married. You must appoint two sales people, and you only visit the really important customers.'

'I fear you are right as usual Trudi. I have to recover, the Professeur said that they had saved me this time, but another attack might be different. I am to take regular exercise, plain food, just a little alcohol.'

'And sex? Is that exercise?'

'I will ask.'

'Rousse is one of my teachers so I would rather he did not know our relationship. He just thinks I am your protégé. So be careful please.'

'Of course. They say I can go home in about three days if everything is well.'

'I think you should go to the Château. The air is clean and you can walk and ride. I will come at weekends. I am going to make sure that you do as you are told. I know that you like to be in control, but this time Trudi is the boss. Can Gérard help. What does he do? What about Sabine? Could she do something more than teach me riding and groom horses?' Who could you promote at the salon? You can think about these things. I am going to the salon today, to tell them how you are, so they are not worried and nor are you.'

'There is one worry. We are not married. I know you have said July next year, but if I should die, I want you to look after my children and pass to them my inheritance. I want us to have a secret civil wedding, the only legal way in France. I do not trust anyone else to look after the babies.'

I thought it over. If it could be secret, then it made sense. 'Then have an official wedding next year? White dress and hundreds of guests?'

'Of course.'

'Can it be secret?

'Oh yes. I can guarantee that.'

'Where?'

'At the Château or Alençon.'

'Have I time to think about this?'

'Of course, as long as you like, but not eighteen months.'

'Simon I will decide soon. It is now Wednesday. Within a week you will have my answer. Now I must go to class and I will go to the Maison this afternoon. I will be back this evening. Now you rest. Do as they tell you.'

I kissed him, my Simon, my dear Simon. My problems had just multiplied.

That afternoon I went to Maison Beauvonne. I spoke to Jacques and Thomas. I asked if there was anyone they could recommend as a salesperson to cover the World? They said they would think about it. Thomas suggested the best thing to do was poach someone and the way to do it was employ head hunters. I said I would see to it. They also said that they needed a director on site. They were busy with designs, all the work entailed in design and making frocks. They hadn't time or expertise to run the Maison. I promised to ask the head hunters to look into that too. I went around the floor talking to the staff in ones and twos or more, repeating the bulletin on Simon, time and again, shaking hands, kissing cheeks, making them all feel secure and valued, even down to the latest apprentice.

I took a taxi to the apartment and found my friends home. I suggested we go to Franco's again. I needed a shot of pasta to get me through this latest crisis.

This time I did not break down, although Franco was again touchy feely and all commiserations. I saw Simon later. Annette and Gérard were there and I asked them to wait while I told Simon of my visit to the Maison. I collected

Gérard and Annette and took them to Willi's bar. We found a table relatively out of the way.

'I know,' I said, 'about Catherine.'

'We tried, Simon tried, reasoning with her. Her death was unfortunate.' Gérard said.

'I know that was you I spoke to on Simon's phone that day, Gérard. So tell me everything. I know Simon left the Château and then went back. Why, what happened? I will be quite frank with you. Simon feels insecure from his heart attack, fearful of another and leaving three orphans. He has asked me to marry him in secret, so they are properly, legally looked after.

'I am willing, more than willing. It is what I want, because I love him very much. But I must know exactly what happened and why?'

'I see it is no use keeping the secret any longer.'

'Oh it will be a secret, just the four of us, But I know enough not to be lied to. I was planning to have this out with Simon when I was called to the hospital. Tell me now.'

'Very well Trudi. This is what happened. That weekend, Catherine told Simon that she was going to divorce him and ask for sole custody of the children on the grounds that he was never there and she would be citing you as correspondent. She had found all his photos of you and Simon together, on the bateaux, at the races, skiing. She and that bitch Françoise told him that he was as good as finished. She would take the Château and the children. You and Simon would be plastered all over the newspapers. There was a terrible row and those two women just laughed in his face.

'Françoise was scheduled to take the children to the doctor for their injections. Catherine had a hair appointment in Alençon. Simon sent me south with his phone in his car, and he sat in my car, out of the way, waiting for her to go to the hairdresser. When she was gone, he planned to return, stage a robbery in which he would take all her jewellery and the photos and if she protested he would be able to say he was a hundred miles away.

'As with most plans involving humans, something went awry. Simon returned on foot through the forest, expecting the house to be empty. He went to Catherine's room and took her jewel box and emptied the safe. The photos and all the negatives and memory cards were in her dressing table, under her lingerie. He took them. He was leaving her room when she came up the stairs. Her appointment had been cancelled and she had returned. He barged past her, hoping that the plan would still work, his word against hers, and because I had his phone and a call was coming through from New York, he would be able to prove he was miles away. She yelled and shouted at him, even as he ran out of the door. She must have attempted to run down the stairs after him and tripped. He never knew of her death until you broke it to him.

'He was in a disturbed state. He drove to me, meeting me twenty minutes ahead of schedule, so he must have driven like the wind. I gave him his phone and we swapped cars. I drove north, he drove south. I wondered why she had not attempted to phone him, but of course she was already dead. Simon just shrugged, said he did not care if she phoned or not. He drove off, and of course, crashed. You know the rest.

'I was so surprised to get your phone call, I didn't even attempt to sound like Simon. I am not sorry for Catherine. She played a good hand but badly. She really wasn't interested in the children and Françoise was an awful nanny. Simon was frightened the children would be ruined and you and he would be dragged through the scandal sheets.

'So, that is all. His accident and Catherine's death were the end of a terrible twelve months. What are you going to do?'

'I am not going to do anything. You do not tell Simon that I know this. This secret goes with us to the grave. You both understand me?'

'Of course. I think you have made the right, the only decision.'

'Now Gérard. Tell me what you do?'

'Well, I'm sort of odd job. When Simon wants something done, then I do it, run errands, messages, look after things.'

'Have you qualifications?'

'I'm trained as an accountant.'

'So how do you make a living?'

'Simon makes me an allowance. Annette is the real earner.'

'I want you to work at the Salon de Couture, Maison Beauvonne. I will arrange a salary for you, more than the allowance, but you will be there everyday. You will not be in charge of anyone or anything, but it will be your job to administer the day to day running of the business, Booking halls for shows, ordering and buying at best possible price, materials etc., booking models for the shows as required by the designers. You have six months to get to grips, then I will decide with Simon whether you stay. I want you to be a success. It is up to you. I think you can do it. If you need a professional buyer then I will advertise for one. I am already advertising via head-hunters for a fashion salesman. I was going to advertise the post I am giving you.

'You Annette, I want you to put Beauvonne on the map. Keep it in the news. For a start, a heart rending story about the curse of Beauvonne, Simon's illness being the latest in the saga. The history, the death of his brother, the early death of his parents, Catherine's death, his crash, his heart attack. The Beauvonne curse. When we appoint a salesman I want the world to know. I want regular updates on Simon's return to health. I want you to make sure that every fashion journalist and fashionista and important customer attends the shows, pop stars, film stars, sports stars, anyone with money. If we need a bigger building, then find one, but beat them down on price. Submit a guest list to me and I will check it over with Simon.

'Simon will not be well enough to make decisions for at least two months. I want him to just get well and not worry about Maison Beauvonne. I want you both to work hard and help me keep this ship afloat and there will be a bonus. I will keep an eye on things, but it is down to you. We are depending on you to do your best, so we all get rich.

'OK, I am getting a taxi home. Can I drop you somewhere?'

We found a taxi. I dropped them at Annette's apartment. They promised to do their best. I was surprised that they did not question my authority.

I went back to Uni next day and saw Simon in the evenings until he was transferred to the Château. I employed a nurse to make sure he did not cheat on his recovery programme.

Friday night, I drove to the Château. What a good present the Mercedes had been, because now I was becoming a weekend commuter and the big fast car ate up the miles effortlessly.

I found Simon sitting comfortably in the salon. He attempted to rise when I entered, but I stayed him with a gesture and bent and we kissed. The nurse made a discreet exit. I said I must go and see Sophie and the children.

Sophie was well and so were the children apparently, for they were all in bed and asleep. I peeped in. Sophie was putting their clothes away and clearing up the toys before coming down to dinner. I went to my room, had a quick shower and did my face and dressed in an aqua tea dress.

We were just four for dinner and it was an everyday affair, vegetable soup, chicken in a parsley sauce and chocolate mousse. We did not drink wine as Simon was still considered to be an invalid. As soon as it was over, the nurse insisted that Simon go to bed. He had walked out in the grounds today for the first time and she considered, in spite of his protests, that he was tired. Tomorrow Annette and Gérard would arrive and we would all have a conference and find out what was going on. When Simon was settled, I went in and kissed him goodnight. He wanted me to stay but I excused myself, saying I had work to do.

I walked down to see Sabine. Together we walked to the top of the small hill the other side of the village. The dusk was just settling gently over a warm June day. Insects buzzed, and far off I heard a cuckoo call. We sat on a grassy bank.

'Will you ride with me tomorrow,' I asked.

'Of course. Then perhaps Sunday, I can come to Paris with you. Will that be all right?'

'It will be super. Stay the week and return with me next Friday.'

'That will be great Trudi. So you still wear the ring?"

'Oh yes. I heard an explanation from Gérard and Annette. I am not sure that it was the whole truth. Almost certainly not, and it annoys me that they think they can lie to me, but in the end, I am not bothered.

'Sabine, I need you to promise me that you will never tell a soul about what you saw. I beg you, and I know it is much to ask. Catherine was planning to ruin Simon and take the Château and the children. Whatever happened, occurred because of that. Whether she fell or was pushed down the stairs, I cannot tell, but it is true that at that time, when you saw Simon running through the forest, she was not supposed to be at the Château. She should have been having a hairdo, but it was cancelled at the last minute. Therefore, I do not think that her death was premeditated. It is what I have thought about all week. Can you give me your word?

'Of course. I would not have told anyone in any case. I'm glad she is dead.'

'I have taken control of Simon's affairs at the moment, the Maison Beauvonne, and the estate. Gérard now has a proper job to do, and I will make sure he does it or he is out, cousin or no. Annette I like very much but has been I feel, lazy. I hope to have sharpened her up.

'The next thing is the estate here. You know it well, and you know farming. Can you give me some ideas of what to do. If you were running it, what would you do.'

'Much. OK, we have to keep some parkland, but you could run sheep on that. Then there is a lot of land that just seems waste. It needs tidying up and being made productive.'

'But what about the wild life? We would not want to deprive animals and birds of refuge.'

'Of course not. That low land which is so boggy, I would like to make that into a lake. We could use the soil taken out to raise the level of those meadows, and it would be a wildlife paradise for duck and geese. Then the forest wants attention, take some timber out, to make room for the healthiest trees and to pay for it. And there is some replanting to do too. There are grants available. Then we have to look at the rotations. I think we can improve the land with some modern crops, flax, rape, peas and beans which we grow but the estate doesn't.'

'Does this take a lot of money?'

'No, not too much.'

'Sabine, I would like you to walk the estate and make a plan. Then I want proper costings and estimated returns. We will pay you for your time. If we like what you propose, then I would give you the job of Estate manager. What do you say?'

'You could advertise the post and get someone with a proven record.'

'But I would not know them. I want to have people about us that are friends. You would also be, to be honest, cheaper than an imported expert, at least to start with, but eventually we would expect to pay the going rate.'

'I will come to Paris with you, then the next week I will make a proper survey with the estate map and make proposals Trudi. It will be a dream come true and put my studies to good use.'

'Good, I am delighted. Now there is one other thing that I have to tell you, another secret. Simon has premonitions of an early death. Of course I think he is wrong, but one never knows. He is frightened that his children will not be looked after and will somehow be disinherited. Before the crise cardiaque, he had as you know, asked me to marry him and I said in eighteen months time, but agreed to be engaged. Now he wants to marry me for the sake of the children. I have agreed to a secret wedding immediately, to give him peace of mind and an official wedding next year. Next year I would like you to be my chief bridesmaid. Will you please?'

'Oui mon amie Trudi, bien sur.' We kissed.

'I have not told Simon yet, I am telling him tomorrow. But we will not announce our wedding for another six months, a decent time after Catherine's death and giving Simon recovery time.'

We walked through the village and she came to the estate gate with me. 'Till tomorrow.' She said.

I went to bed happy that another gap had been filled.

Gérard and Annette arrived just as I was dismounting Sheba. I put her in the stable and saw to her needs and went in to change. We all shared a nice lunch of lobster salad with a bottle of Gewürztraminer from Alsace. I asked Gérard how his work had gone. He said he had been very busy, booking venues, driving down prices and progress chasing orders for materials, some of which were very difficult to get hold of. I asked whether he needed a buyer, but he stated that at present he didn't. If the readymade took off and the factory in the Auvergne came into being then it would need a buyer.

Annette showed me the week's papers. She had managed everyday to get something in regarding Beauvonne, even if it was only a bulletin on Simon's recovery. This weekend, she said, she wanted Simon to give a full account of his heart attack and she would have it in Le Monde, Le Figaro and Paris-Match.

She produced a list of people to invite to the shows that Simon promised to look over.

The meeting broke up. I took Simon out for a drive to the coast and we walked along the sea front, giving his nurse time off over the weekend.

The breeze off the sea was quite warm, the sun rather hazy. Gulls cried and screams from children far off were the only sounds. We sat on the promenade in the warmth. I told him of everything I had done and asked for his approval. He thought I had done well. His one dispute was over Sabine. I convinced him in the end, after saying that it would be a trial employment and that she understood that.

'So, mon cher homme, when are we to marry?'

'You agree?'

'As soon as possible, but in secret, with a big wedding July next year.'

'That is the best medicine. I feel as excited as a small boy with a new toy. It is a great weight off my mind. Trudi, you have exceeded all my expectations, managing my affairs. Are you doing your own work too, your study?'

'Of course, but if I am to be a wife, I want to be a rich wife, so the business and the estate is important. And you are important too. I want you to live. You cannot do all these things you do. I am looking for a super salesman to take the weight off you, although Professor Rousse says that there is no reason why you should not live into old age. Good food, plenty of vegetables and fruit, not too much alcohol and above all, this lifestyle, rushing around the world all the time, changing time zones, has to stop. You cannot do everything yourself. Now we go home to see the children and for dinner we eat plainly.'

We married in secret two weeks later.

There is another Trudi novel, 'Trudi et Simon.'

Made in the USA
Charleston, SC
10 July 2013